eating bitter

Charles Colyott

This is a work of fiction. All characters, organizations, and events portrayed are products of the author's imagination or used fictitiously.

"Rain Bokeh" by Kevin Dooley is licensed under CC by 4.0 and the original version can be found at https://www.flickr.com

Here's the thing, this isn't going to be some How-Randall-Got-His-Groove-Back midlife crisis tale, and it doesn't involve fearless kung fu warriors engaged in exotic hand-to-hand combat; it isn't a swooning ballad to the love of my life, though I truly hope she features in it. This time there are no suave, wise-cracking good guys, no humorless, drug-addled bad guys.

The story I want to tell you is all about how I learned to sleep at night, to close my eyes without seeing cold places and dead eyes… how I dragged whatever was left of me up out of the dark, finally.

That's the story I want to tell, because that's the story I need to hear.

I want to know how it ends.

Like I said, I haven't been sleeping much lately. On a night like tonight, I get maybe two hours, three tops. Usually it's pain that drags me from sleep, a whole body ache that locks muscle and bone and fuses the vertebrae into a single rigid column. I hurt. I hurt, and I feel old, like some obsolete bit of machinery left to corrode in the sea.

It's been a hell of a year. Well, a few years.

…Okay, fine, the better part of a decade.

On a night like tonight, when the soft blanket of sleep is ripped away and reality snaps into focus, when my muscles cramp violently enough to make me wonder if the tendons might tear themselves free from bone with the force of it, I start to question the wisdom of my decision to give up booze.

Some nights – the bad ones – I wake up alone, back at my place. Lately, those nights are, thankfully, rarer than they once were. Tracy has been doing well in therapy, meditation has done wonders, and Faith has helped to bring us closer again. She still has her moments… Hell, she has entire days… but she works really hard. She shouldn't have to, and that kills me. But, as Cheng says, "One cannot regret having been a stupid, useless assholehead all of one's life. One can only endeavor not to be a stupid, useless assholehead today."

This assholehead has been two hundred sixty-nine days without incident.

Tonight it wasn't the pain that woke me. Tonight it was a nine pound ball of rage dressed in a tiny nightgown Tracy made from a RAC concert shirt. Tracy appeared to be sleeping well, for once, so I slipped quietly from the bed and scooped Faith up from her crib as quickly as I could. She fit quite comfortably against the right side of my chest, and as she nuzzled against my shirt, her cries intensified once she realized that I didn't possess the anatomical equipment she was interested in.

She reevaluated my usefulness after I gave her a bottle.

I turned out the lights and eased into one of Tracy's hand-painted kitchen chairs while Faith drank greedily. One of her tiny hands settled on the back of my own hand and stayed there. I was so startled and transfixed by the image, lit only by a bit of streetlight spilling in through the windows, that I didn't immediately notice the larger, fleshier, and wrinklier ball of rage that had crept up onto my lap beside her.

Tito still wasn't too sure about the baby, and I wasn't too sure about allowing Tito around her, either. Tracy insisted that he wouldn't hurt her, but I thought that could just be her own irrational bias. Or, possibly, a testament to his satanic mental powers.

At that moment, though, I didn't have any free hands with which to remove the fleshy creature, so I kept an eye on him. I figured that, if nothing else, I could just stand up abruptly if he looked like he might do something evil to my kid.

Tito looked up at me, yellow eyes reflecting the streetlight, and then he locked onto Faith. He craned his neck out to her, sniffing audibly a few times, and then pointedly turned his back on her, coiled himself into a ball, and promptly fell asleep. I couldn't help noticing that he'd coiled suspiciously close to Faith. That he had, in fact, flopped in such a way that he was pressing his peach fuzz-

4

covered side against her, and that the pinkish tentacle of his tail just happened to twine around the baby's ankle.

***

I sent the invitations out a few weeks ago. Invitations and phone calls and other arrangements. It all felt very grown up, very alien to me.

I'd managed to get the venue on short notice, which was a surprise. Spring and summer were usually booked solid, but we were lucky enough to catch them on the morning of a cancellation. That, combined with the manager recognizing me from one of the endless news shows that had aired after the Wycombe, Francis, & Associates affair. No matter how much I declined their requests for an interview, the reporters kept coming around. I didn't want my name and face plastered everywhere, but evidently they didn't care and there wasn't much I could do about it.

Land of the free, my ass.

Anyway, it got us in. And a ten percent discount.

So all the pain and terror and the ensuing bullshit was worth it, I guess.

The hall was supposed to be historic. I'm not really sure why. All I knew was that it was beautiful, it was the right size, and the location was decent, nestled as it was into one of Tracy's favorite parks.

I'd gotten a snarky RSVP from Tony, which was fine, though he said everything hinged on Daniel and his health. I didn't much like the sound of that. It had been almost a year. I knew that Daniel had been hurt. He'd been hurt bad. But hell, so had I. And I was fine.

Right?

I called them one day, while Tracy was out shopping with her mother and Faith slept in her crib. I didn't like being there, essentially, alone. After everything, the apartment still felt like her space, and without her there to animate it, the place felt wrong somehow, unwelcoming.

"So. What the hell?" I said, when Tony answered.

"What?"

"The wishy-washy response. What's going on with Daniel? The

last I heard, he was on-board with all of this."

Tony sighed. "Hold on," he said.

I heard him walking, heard a door. Then the crackle and hiss of wind on the mouthpiece of Tony's phone.

"Sorry," Tony said, after closing the door. "He's paranoid that I'm always talking about him…"

"…Can't imagine why," I said with a grin.

"Listen, Randall… he's…not doing so well. You know we'd love to come. You know that…"

"What's going on? Is he doing what I told him to do?"

We'd done some Skype calls a few weeks back, and I'd shown Daniel some basic instructions to practice a type of static qigong that would help build his strength back up. Predictably, the Brazilian badass who was used to doing one-armed cartwheels and spinning heel kicks, just stared at me as I tried to teach him the benefits of standing really still in goofy positions for long periods of time… until he tried it. Then, when he was only able to hold the basic position for half a minute, he did something I never expected him to do. He hung up on me and wouldn't talk to me for a week. During that time, Tony had said that Daniel practiced as often as he could manage, but only succeeded in building up to about five minutes of standing per session. I told him that it took time, especially recovering from the kind of injuries that Daniel had sustained. He'd had both of his legs broken just below the knees by a B movie karate guy who had been whacked out on the drug that had been the bane of my existence for the last year or so: Jade.

On the other end of the line, Tony was silent for a minute.

"No," he said, finally. "He's not. He quit. He doesn't sleep, Randall. Hardly eats. Won't leave that goddamned wheelchair. I had to pay extra to hire a physical therapist to make house calls because he just decided one day that he wasn't going to leave the house. If he had his way, he would just wheel up to the windows and zone out, staring at the beach."

"Any change in his medication?" I said.

"No, just an anti-inflammatory, Vicodin for pain, Zoloft…"

I went to the fridge and got a coke, then froze for a second because I thought I heard Faith. It turned out to simply be new parent paranoia.

"Get him out here, and I'll try to help him out, okay, Tony?"

"What could you do, Randall?"

I sighed. "Well, I realize it hasn't been my primary occupation lately, but I am sort of a doctor, Tony."

"It *is* easy to forget that."

"Yeah… I know."

"I'll try, okay?"

"Trace and I would love to see you guys."

"I'll try."

Once we were off the phone, I decided not to be a giant hypocrite and do some qigong myself. It was easy to get on Daniel's case, but I really hadn't been doing everything I could to help myself, either. *Zhan Zhuang,* the standing qigong that had been the foundation training of my Tai Chi and the exercise I'd recommended to Daniel, was simple. And deceptively difficult. As a young, strong, and healthy kid, I'd been astounded by how tough, and how painful, the training had been. These days, well, I didn't know how good I'd had it as a kid, I'll tell you that much.

I assumed the basic stance: feet shoulder-width apart, knees bent a little and tailbone tucked, as if sitting on the edge of a stool, and arms forming a relaxed circle. The posture was called 'Embracing the tree.' Tracy called it, "That weird tree-hugger shit."

I grinned at the memory, but the grin quickly faded. Those had been better days, the days before the pain, back when we'd been together. Really together. Everything was tainted now, however much we both wanted to pretend that it wasn't. The way I would pretend not to see how she flinched when I made any movement toward her. Or how we could only sleep together in the same bed if she took enough sedatives to drop an elephant. And what a leap of faith that had to be for her, to take those drugs and relinquish control, not knowing if she would ever wake again. Dramatic? Maybe, but deep down, on a level that she would never admit to, those were the thoughts going through her head.

I'd almost killed her, after all, and I'd done it with a cheerful smile plastered on my face.

That kind of thing leaves a mark.

I felt a renewed sympathy for Daniel at the ten minute mark of my own session. The puckered, waxen scar in the center of my left palm throbbed in time with my heartbeat, sending needles of pain all down the arm, which felt swollen and suddenly, inexplicably heavy. In response, I could feel my postural muscles adjust. My phasic muscles weren't with the program, though, and that sent new waves of pain through my body as my not-quite-healed abs clenched.

Not so long ago I would've rewarded myself with an icy cold beer if I could just push through the pain and make it through the session. An icy cold beer is a hell of a reward.

These days...

I thought about the contents of Tracy's fridge, the flat two liter bottle of Coke, the two day old Chinese takeout. I frowned. I remembered that there was a quarter sleeve of Girl Scout cookies in the cabinet, but that just didn't have the same power as the beer.

I sighed. "Oh, screw this..." I mumbled to myself and allowed my hands to sink down to my sides. If I'd been a good boy, I would've gone on to work a bit on my Tai Chi form.

I was not a good boy.

I walked down the step into Tracy's living room and dropped into a surly slouch on her overstuffed violet sofa. I'd just picked up the remote control to turn on the TV when I heard the front door.

Tracy came in, heavily laden with bags, and I quickly stood to help her. There it was again, the tiniest recoil on her part, the wide eyes, the *fear*, and low in my gut, just behind the old gunshot wound, something twisted.

"Can I help?" I said.

Tracy looked away and said, "Sure! You could, um, put these things in the nursery."

She set the bags down on the couch, several feet away from me, and stepped away. She had her good days and bad days. This, clearly, wasn't going to be one of the good ones. And because fate just loves to stick it in and break it off, I looked up to see Tracy's mom, Genevieve, coming in with even more bags. Her eyes met mine, briefly, and she said, "Doctor Lee."

After all this time, after Faith and everything, I was still "Doctor Lee."

Giving up booze had definitely been a bad idea.

"So...What's all this?" I said.

Trace was in the kitchen, unpacking a shopping bag filled with what appeared to be every conceivable type of bottle known to man. "Stuff," she said. "So much stuff. Because my mother is a crazy person."

Genevieve was setting down her bags just inside the door and said, "Well, I want my granddaughter to have everything she needs, that's all."

I flashed her a smile. I had a not-so-sneaking suspicion that Tracy's parents hated me with the white-hot fury of a thousand suns, but Tracy had always told me I was overreacting. She made me promise to give them the benefit of the doubt, and I did... even when I was sure that every other word they said to me was some kind of veiled slam, each one just another slit in a verbal version of the death of a thousand cuts. Was I really so insecure that I believed that crap?

"It's hard enough, being a single parent. Especially these days," Tracy's mother said.

I think Tracy said, "Single parent?"

I'm not sure because, at the same time, I was saying, "What the hell is *that* supposed to mean?"

Genevieve looked genuinely shocked. A thin, reedy cry issued from the nursery, and, though Tracy was already on her way down the steps from the kitchen to the hall, I said, "I've got her," and went to get Faith.

Faith's room was painted in pink and gold, with the twelve Chinese zodiac animals parading along the walls in Tracy's signature cartoonish style. Faith was wedged into a back corner of her crib, her neck at an awkward angle, her cheeks blotchy with impotent baby rage and her tiny fists raised in protest.

"How did you end up over there?" I said in Mandarin. I usually spoke to Faith in Mandarin. I figured that she'd get her English from Tracy with no problem, but I always liked the idea of raising a little polyglot (When Grace, my first child, was in kindergarten, the teacher would ask her to count to ten, and Gracie would say, "In English, Mandarin, Cantonese, or Japanese?" Her teacher thought she was being a little smart ass and sent her to the principal's office). Tracy's parents were *certain* that this would screw up Faith's ability to learn English, and they usually added in something like, "Doesn't she have enough struggles already without adding in *this* burden?"

They were both educators and used to having their expertise

accepted without question. Since I'd had the gall to point out that neither of them were linguistics experts – and that neither of them had experience with language acquisition beyond English – I'd earned myself a free lifetime supply of disapproving scowls.

She had settled down a bit by the time I took her back out to the living room. I'm not sure what had happened in the short time I'd been gone, but the room had a distinctly icy feel to it and Tracy was standing well within her mother's personal space, flashing her a look of extreme displeasure. Having been on the receiving end of that look many times, I didn't envy her... but hey, better her than me.

Ignoring the tension of a Sandovalian stand-off, I said, "She managed to roll herself into a corner."

Tracy turned from her mother, her expression changing to one of delight. "Really?"

I nodded.

Faith hiccupped.

Tracy came over and gently cupped the back of our daughter's tiny head and leaned down to kiss her forehead. "You made it all the way to the corner all by yourself? All by yourself you did that?" she whispered to Faith. "Mommy's strong little girl."

Faith had grown a lot, but she was still smaller at three months than some babies are at birth. Consequently, we made an extra big deal out of the little moments that suggested that she was on the right track, that she would someday grow to be "normal," whatever the hell that was. Genevieve loomed over Tracy's shoulder, her own tight-lipped sneer replaced with a look of amazement and joy. It took a minute before I realized that her hand was on my shoulder.

One little gesture. A recognition that I was a human being, a father, a part of her daughter's life... and then it was gone. I don't know if she even realized she'd done it.

Genevieve's eyes met mine and she said, "Could I..?"

I gently passed Faith to her. She cradled my daughter in the crook of her arm and gazed down at her. I glanced at Tracy, but she was watching her mother.

Genevieve's eyes went from Faith to Tracy to me.

"Why don't the two of you let me watch the baby for awhile?" she said.

"Mom, it's okay. There's so much stuff to put away…" Tracy said.

"It'll still be here when you get back. Go to lunch, catch a movie or something… You deserve a break."

Tracy looked to me. I shrugged.

She took a few minutes to get ready, but then Tracy gave her mother a hug, told her thanks, and kissed Faith goodbye. The way I figured it, Genevieve and I were about a billion light years away from hugging status, but I mirrored her and cautiously put a hand on her shoulder while I kissed Faith goodbye. On the way out the door I told her, sincerely, thank you.

***

I let Tracy pick the restaurant. We ended up at this street taco place on Delmar. She had fish tacos, and I tried their roast duck tacos. The weather, especially for Saint Louis in late June, was atypically beautiful, so we sat outside and listened to the sounds of the city.

"Is it wrong that I really, really want a beer?" Tracy said.

I shook my head. I'd been thinking the same thing.

"We could split one," I said.

Tracy rolled her eyes. "What would be the point of that?"

I shrugged.

A beautiful day spent with a beautiful woman should be a celebration. Especially when one is madly in love with that beautiful woman. Especially when both parties should be extremely grateful to be alive and whole and together still, after everything that has happened to them.

We could have lost so much.

But what we *had* lost was enough to ruin everything.

And the truth was that I still didn't know how to get it back. Or, even, if I *could.*

"You look like shit," she said.

"Sorry," I said.

Tracy furrowed her brow and said, "You don't have to apologize. Have you thought about seeing someone? About the sleep thing?"

"Who would I see?"

"Um… I dunno… a *doctor*, maybe?"

"I am a doctor, Trace."

She rolled her eyes. "You *know* what I meant, Randall. I'm not disparaging your skills. I'm just saying that sometimes pharmaceuticals are a magical thing."

I took a swig of ice cold water.

Water.

Ugh.

Fish fuck in this, I thought.

"I'll pass," I said.

Tracy scooped a bite of roasted corn onto the tines of her plastic fork. She seemed to study it for a long while before saying, "Are you ever going to tell me about it?"

"About not sleeping? There's not much to tell and what there is isn't terribly interesting: Most people do it. Lately, I don't. The End."

She sighed.

"*Randall,*" was all she said, but what I heard in that single word was, "Don't be an asshole. You know what I mean. Tell me what happened when we were apart. Tell me what happened in that horrible place. Tell me about *her.*"

I took a deep breath and let it out slowly. "Trace… It's not really something that I want to talk about, and I'm not sure that it's really anything you want to hear."

She set her fork down.

"Look, I know that everything's fucked, okay, Randall? And I know that some of that is my fault–"

"No, Trace–"

"Shush. Everything used to be so easy and comfortable and wonderful. And I think part of the reason they were is because you and I could say anything to each other. Everything was open. My therapist says that I have to be willing to tell you the things that I don't ever want to tell you, like when I'm… a-afraid. Of you." She swallowed hard and continued, "A-And she says that you have to be willing to just listen to those things. And be supportive. She says that we have to be able to communicate these things."

I drank some more.

…Water.

"Whatever happened..? It hurt you, Randall. And that kills me.

You have this… this *haunted* look and it breaks my heart. I want to help you, Randall. That's all. I just want to help."

I didn't doubt that, but I also couldn't help thinking that wasn't her only concern. This wasn't her first attempt to get me to talk, and I always got the feeling that it wasn't so much that she wanted to hear about the horrors I saw and experienced, but the hot blonde I experienced them with.

Was I being unfair?

Possibly.

Was I stupid enough to tell her my theory?

Hell no.

"What would you like to know?" I said, instead.

"I want to know what happened. I want to hear it from you, not from the news. I know that things were bad, but it might help you to talk about it."

I really needed a beer.

I took a bite of duck taco instead. It was fantastic.

"You have to try this, Tracy. Seriously."

I looked up in time to see the hurt scowl on her face.

I set down the taco.

"What do you want me to say, Trace? That a guy I hardly knew, a guy who spent his life saving kids from real, honest-to-god monsters, got himself killed just to protect me? That he's the guy, the real hero, who should be on the news? Or would you rather hear about the night I spent hiding in a swamp, terrified that I was going to die? There are things out there that you can't un-see, Trace, and that's what I saw. I saw things that never go away. And they're right there, every time I close my eyes. Things that would give you nightmares for the rest of your life just to hear about them, and I don't want that for you."

Her eyes were wide.

A few people sitting at the other tables were staring at us.

I, apparently, had lost control of the volume knob on my voice unit.

Oops.

Tracy reached across the table and took my hand, her fingers tentative. It wasn't until she touched me that I realized my hands were shaking.

Quieter, this time, I said, "I used to think that people are basically good. They could be selfish or greedy or scared, and that might make them do bad things, but underneath it all there was a basic decency. But these people... They weren't people, even though they looked like the rest of us. You could look into their eyes, and there was just *nothing* there. They weren't selfish and they weren't scared. They weren't mentally ill, though I'm sure that's what the shrinks would say. They were just... *evil*. I don't know any other way to put it. You can't do the things they did to people – to children – for fun or for money or any of it, and be a human being."

She squeezed my hand. It happened to be the hand she'd put a bullet through, the one that had mostly healed and rarely hurt at all anymore... at least until beautiful, sexy women with a surprisingly strong grip gave it an encouraging, supportive, bone-readjusting squoosh. Then it hurt quite a lot, actually. I clenched my jaws to avoid making what would almost certainly be an unmanly distress sound.

Instead I focused on her eyes. They were wonderful and warm and alive, and the promise I saw there made the pain go away, cheesy as that may sound.

I had the briefest flash of the Plastic Man's raw red lidless eyes. Cold and soulless eyes.

"They wanted to make me watch what they were going to do to that little girl. And there was nothing I could do about it. Nothing. And if you and Cheng had shown up any later, they would have."

Tracy leaned across the table and kissed my forehead. "It's okay now, Randall," she said.

"No," I said. "It's not."

I lowered my voice and said, "I... killed them, Tracy. I fucking *murdered* them."

Tracy glanced around us nervously and said, "Shhh, it's okay, Randall. You did what you had to do to protect yourself and those kids."

"No, you don't understand, Trace... Whatever I did to them? It wasn't enough. There wasn't anything that I could do to them that could ever be enough. Sometimes, when I can't sleep, I think about Bertolt, and how it would've felt to hold his head in my hands and to watch his eyes fill with fear at the realization that *he wasn't going to fucking get away with it* anymore. And I wonder how it would've felt to just push my fingers through his eyes and to hear him scream, even for just a second. But it… it would've been over too quickly. There wasn't anything I could do to him – to any of them – that would ever be *enough.*"

"You wanted them to suffer the way they made others suffer," she said.

"I wanted them to pay for what they are. I wanted to hurt them. I enjoyed hurting them. And if you really want to know what keeps me up at night, it's that."

Tracy said nothing, but her hand was still in mine and surely that said something. After the Jade and everything, to still be here after hearing that I had enjoyed inflicting pain… I'm sure her shrink would have had something to say about that.

My throat was dry. I took another drink.

Blech.

"The only consolation I have, I suppose, is that I *could've* given in. Beatrix did. And I think about her sometimes, too, and what it must be like to feel that kind of hate all the time. I could've been that, too, I think. It was right there, closer to me than we are right now. It's still there, though it's…quieter now."

"Beatrix. Was she blonde I found you with?"

I nodded.

I told Tracy about her, really told her about Bea, for the first time. How we met, how we fled into the swamp together. How I found out about who – and what – she was, and the circumstances that can turn a girl into something like the Harlequin. When I was finished, Tracy flagged down our waiter. A few minutes later, he reappeared and set the glass in the neutral space between us on the table.

At first, neither of us touched it.

"It's just the one," Tracy said. "Just the one, and we're sharing it."

I nodded.

She reached out and picked up the beer. Her small hand made a ghostly print in the frosty glass as she took a long, slow sip.

"Sweet Jesus, that's good," she said, sliding it over to me.

I stared at the drink. My fingers fit comfortably alongside Tracy's phantom fingers on the icy surface of the glass.

I drank.

It was good.

Better than the ice water. Better than all the ice water, ever.

I was setting the glass on the table top when Tracy said, "So… knowing what she was… you still let her go?"

"Beatrix?" I said.

"Who else?" she said.

I nodded.

"Why?" she said. Her head was cocked at an endearing angle, with her raven hair falling just so around her face. I looked down from her to the drink, the taste of the beer still in my mouth. I took another deep breath.

"I don't know, exactly," I said, though that wasn't really true. I think a part of me couldn't reconcile the girl I knew with the kind of sadistic monster that the Harlequin was known to be. Maybe that was it, initially. Maybe I wanted to believe that Bea wasn't *really* capable of that sort of thing. Maybe. But there was a more selfish part of me, deep down, who *wanted* her out there, doing the things I couldn't do. That part, the me I don't want to admit I see when I look in the mirror, recognized a kindred spirit in the quirky blonde with the body of a porn star and the mind of a psychopath.

Except, that wasn't fair either.

I've done bad things. More than I could list off. I have taken lives, and not always in self defense. I'm not proud of it, though, and I never took joy in it.

Liar, liar. Pants on fire…

"Randall?"

I looked up at Tracy.

"Did you hear me?"

"No. I'm sorry."

Tracy's cheeks colored.

"Sorry. I zoned out there for a sec," I said.

Tracy took the glass. This time she did more than sip. There was perhaps a quarter of the beer left when she was done, and this made me sadder than I'd care to admit.

"I said, Randall… I said… Did you… have feelings for her?"

Aha, I thought. *The real question, at last.*

"No, Trace. It wasn't like that."

Her eyes met mine, and she smiled a little.

"Were you jealous? Is that what all this was about?"

"No! Nothing like that. I told you, I was worried about you."

"Yeah, but you were also worried about her, right?"

"Shut up and drink the rest of that before I do. Asshole."

A few days later, I sat in a California Pizza Kitchen, nursing a Coke and waiting for someone to drop off my bill. Tracy was back at her place, and I was thinking about her and how things had changed.

That was life, though, eh?

One minute you're madly in love with a gorgeous, tattooed beauty who can't keep her hands off you, and the next minute you're–

Cheng Xin, sitting across the small table from me, belched. Loudly.

–and the next minute you're smelling a ninety year old man's fermented vegetable-scented burps in an airport pizza joint.

"You could say, 'Excuse me,' you know?" I said.

Cheng glanced up, puzzled. "Why?"

"Everybody heard that."

The old man waved a hand dismissively. "Natural bodily function. Should I excuse myself for breathing as well?"

"If your breathing was disgusting and rude, sure."

Cheng frowned. He sniffed loudly and stole a limp fry from my plate. Then, mumbling to himself, I thought I heard him say, "*Your* breathing is disgusting and rude."

I sighed and checked my watch. With no server in sight, I pulled some cash from my wallet and left it on the table. It was more than enough to cover the bill.

Cheng eyed the money and said, "Interesting strategy for good tips: ignore customers."

"What do you want me to do, stiff her?"

"I said nothing."

"Okay, then. They should've landed by now, so come on."

Cheng stood slowly, stretched, and nodded. I glanced at the flight info and walked over to check the arrivals board. I took out my phone and sent a quick text to Tony. Five minutes later, I received a reply.

Cheng and I took the elevator down to the baggage claim and waited. The area seemed strangely desolate considering it was a beautiful early summer day, but a few travelers passed by us, including a family with – if I counted right – seventeen young children and an old man in a motorized chair who seemed hell-bent on running over my foot. Cheng shuffled past and eased himself into a chair just across the way from the baggage carousel.

I caught sight of Tony and raised a hand to wave.

Then I saw Daniel.

The man I saw before me was utterly unrecognizable to the man I had known. He had looked pretty rough during our Skype calls, but even that was an improvement over what I now saw. The thin, ashen man slumping in the wheelchair looked more than just sickly, he looked frail. His trademark braids were gone, and his hair had been shorn close to the skull. His clothes no longer fit. He looked like he could really use a shower. With the dark sunglasses he wore, it was impossible to tell if he was disinterested in his surroundings or if he had passed out.

I crossed over to them and, after brief hellos, helped Tony with their luggage while he wheeled Daniel. "We gotta stop meeting like this," I said, to which Tony replied, "Yes. You should come out and visit us again. This city depresses me a bit, I'm sorry to say."

"Aw, c'mon," I said. "You have so many fond memories of this place."

***

Later that evening, after secreting away our out of town guests, I stopped off at Din Ho Grocery for a minute, talked with a guy about a thing – yes, I'm being coy, but we'll get back to that – and then swung by Tracy's. She didn't know what was up, but I'd told her that I needed her to sign some stuff. Legal stuff. For Faith and all.

She came out of her building dressed in a patterned purple sundress that fell a few inches above the knee, showing just a hint of those world class thighs, and carrying our daughter, who wore a tiny Ramones onesie, a fluffy purple skirt, a skull and crossbones headband, and a suitably matching punk scowl.

My girls.

I hit a button on the console that opened the side door and hopped out of my super-non-cool minivan to help Tracy get Faith settled in her car seat. She beamed at me and kissed me on the cheek when I relieved her of both the miniature anarchist and the miniature anarchist's diaper bag.

Today was one of her good days, which made me very happy. If it had been one of her rough days the evening might've gone down a lot different.

"Hey, you look nice..." she said. I don't do ties, but I was wearing a dark gray suit that still looked halfway decent on me. And I'd actually shaved.

"Oh. You like?"

"Uh, yeah. Duh. You never dress up. So what's this all about?" she said once we were all in and had our seatbelts on.

"Stuff. No biggie," I said.

"Wow. That tells me all kinds of nothing."

"I know... It's not anything to worry about. It's just that my lawyer is in town and I wanted to make sure that we got all the boring paperwork out of the way... stuff like getting you and Faith on my will."

"Ew. Depressing."

"Nah, it'll only take a minute."

This wasn't entirely true. I'd dealt with a lot of the paperwork on my own but, while it was true that there were things that needed her signature – the aforementioned will, for instance – this meeting was really more about getting her acquainted with how things really were. And with how I hoped they would be.

And that all started at the Four Seasons.

It seemed weird to bring Faith's stroller inside, so I carried her in the crook of my arm. She'd fallen asleep again on the short drive, but that was okay. Things would be noisy enough soon, and I wanted to make sure she got her rest.

Lilian met us in the lobby.

"Dr. Lee," she said with a cool, businesslike smile and an extended hand. I shook her hand as if she and I hadn't been working together for twenty years, and said, "Ms. Chow, always a pleasure."

She turned, offering her hand, saying, "And you must be Tracy. Dr. Lee speaks very highly of you."

Tracy shook Lilian's hand and said, "It's nice to meet you."

"Tracy, this is Lilian Chow, my lawyer and accountant."

"Wow. Both? You must've gone to school for a zillion years…" Tracy said. Then her cheeks flushed red and she stared down at her feet.

"Sorry, that was stupid," she said.

Lilian cocked her head and frowned. Then she put a hand on Tracy's shoulder and said, "Perhaps we should get started?"

I followed them into the hotel's restaurant, an Italian place with a name I couldn't pronounce. We sat and Lilian opened her briefcase.

"So… how much stuff is there to sign?" Tracy said, clearly nervous now. I understood perfectly. Lilian scared the shit out of me, too, and I'd known her for a pretty long time. It was like every minute around Lilian was a test that you were always failing. Badly.

I was never sure exactly how she did it, really. She barely cracked five feet in heels and weighed maybe ninety pounds. There was nothing severe about her look. She was, in fact, cute… though I would rather take a cheese grater to my genitals than use that adjective to her face.

"This will only take a few minutes, Miss Sandoval. I assume Dr. Lee informed you about the nature of this visit?"

"…Um… He said it was all…like… wills and stuff?" The words left her lips and she winced. I reached across the table and squeezed her hand. Part of me wished I'd told her in advance, warned her. It wouldn't have helped.

Lilian glanced at me. Just a little glance, but behind that glance was… what?

Disapproval?

Irritation?

Derision?

Check, check, and check.

I may have slumped in my chair a little.

She turned back toward Tracy and said, "Dr. Lee felt it was time to comingle your assets."

"Oh, I think by now our assets have comingled their little brains out," Tracy said with a grin.

Lilian was not amused.

Tracy looked from Lilian to me and back again. After clearing her throat nervously, she said, "I guess… I… don't understand…"

Lilian smiled and slid a sheet of paper across the table to Tracy. "This is a basic financial statement detailing Dr. Lee's – and, now, *your* joint assets."

Tracy stared at the paper. "I… really… don't understand…"

I leaned over and said, "If you look at the bottom of each section that's a total. So then this bottom line over here is sort of all the forms of income and stuff all added together."

Tracy looked up at me again, but the color had faded from her cheeks. All the color that had ever been there, I think.

I started to stand up, thinking that she might faint and that I might need to catch her, but she squeezed her eyes shut tight and took a deep breath.

After a tense, silent minute, she said, "You told me your dad left you some stocks or something…"

"He did," I said.

Lilian cleared her throat and said, "On my advice, Dr. Lee sold off most of his portfolio over the years, using the profits for other investments. When the Great Recession hit Hong Kong, I recommended converting some of those profits to real estate."

Tracy looked back down at the paper. "…But…"

Lilian said, "If you're concerned about those fourth quarter projections, I understand. There are some new taxes on property ownership that are particularly harsh for foreigners, but if you could talk Dr. Lee into looking at some of the tax shelters I've proposed, I think we could mitigate at least some of the damage."

"It's not that…" Tracy said. She looked back at me again. Her eyes welled with tears. I reached out and took her hand.

"What is it?" I said.

Tracy wiped at her eyes and self consciously rubbed her nose. "Is this real? If it's not real, that's okay, but I just… I really need to know. If this is a joke or something it's not funny but whatever. But I need you to tell me, right now."

Lilian said, "Miss Sandoval, I'm not really one for jokes. Frankly, I'm not sure what would even be humorous in this case…"

Tracy picked up the financial statement and shook it as she said, "I just don't understand this. I don't understand what this means, okay?"

Lilian smiled. This time there was nothing intimidating or

mocking to it, only kindness. For once. "It means, Miss Sandoval, that at this time you and Dr. Lee are the tenth wealthiest couple in Hong Kong."

***

Back in the van, shock set in. At least, I think that's what it was. I drove, but every now and then I would look over to see Tracy, frozen, with her hand clasped over her mouth, her eyes wide.

I pulled up to a red light and chanced another look. She still hadn't moved.

"So..." I said. "I probably should have just told you. I just don't know how you say that to someone, really, and I thought it would be a fun surprise but clearly you're upset and I'm sorry for that..."

I was babbling, true, but I didn't know what else to do and it should be pretty apparent by now that babbling is sort of my go to move. Tracy and I had talked about money a few times before, and she never understood why it made me uncomfortable. Don't get me wrong, money is great. But, ultimately, it's just a tool. It's a great tool, but it's still only a tool. My life, so far, has been a bit like trying to construct an infinitely complicated glass sculpture... with a box of crayons and a slice of American cheese. And when people admire your crayons and tell you that your cheese is the bestest cheese that they've ever had, you can't really argue with them.

The difference being that all they needed was to color a picture of a puppy and make a grilled cheese sandwich.

Of course the problem could just be that, whenever I try to explain things to people, I'm complete shit at metaphors and they just end up thinking I'm a dumbass.

Cheese? *Seriously*?

"Trace? C'mon... please talk to me?"

Still nothing.

So I drove. And I continued on with the plan, for whatever good that would do. The sun was low in the sky, finally, and it was beginning to cool off a bit outside, so I rolled down the windows. From the back, Faith made a low cooing sound as she felt the breeze.

The golds and pinks of sunset deepened to indigo as we pulled into the park. And there, lining the walkway, just like they were supposed to, were little paper lanterns glowing with candlelight.

Phew. I love it when a plan comes together.

I looked over at Tracy and then back at Faith before turning off the van and climbing out to get Faith's stroller from the back. Once she was strapped in, I opened the passenger side door and put a hand on Tracy's arm. She turned to look at me and lowered her hands at last. And when I took her hands and helped her out of the car, she saw the lanterns that led off into the park, and she heard the distant music and the laughter and the people.

When her eyes met mine again, she said, "I am going to be so pissed when I wake up from this."

We stepped onto the path. Tracy's hand found mine on the stroller handle and squeezed. I looked into her dark eyes and smiled. Bathed in shadows and candlelight, she was so beautiful. I took her hand in mine and, pushing Faith ahead of us, we followed the path around a corner to where the Spenser House stood. And, waiting for us on the patio, overlooking a placid lily pond, stood pretty much everyone we cared about.

Upon seeing us, they began to applaud and cheer. Faith wasn't sure whether to cry or not, but apparently decided to err on the side of caution. Before she could work herself up, though, Tracy's mother, dressed in a lovely evening gown and wearing actual jewelry (until that moment, I was used to only ever seeing the woman slightly ruffled and with smudges of chalk on her face), crouched down and scooped her up. Tracy's father took a step forward, put an arm around his daughter's shoulders and shook my hand.

From there, things get a little fuzzy. We were swept along a current of well-wishes, stopping only for quick hugs, claps on the back, and handshakes. Tracy's friends were a blur of facial piercings and tattoos, with bearded hipster dudes flashing me ultra casual whassup nods in lieu of the traditional handshake and slinky burlesque dancers wrapping the two of us into weirdly tender three-way hugs. We'd been pulled near the front of the building and, as an old Glen Miller song ended and an Al Green song began, I put an arm around Tracy's waist and directed her eyes to the DJ booth.

She actually gasped and turned to see my reaction, her eyes worried.

"I hired him," I said.

She arched an eyebrow. "... You *did?*"

I nodded.

The DJ caught sight of us, grinned, and said, "Hey, now! Lookin' *fine*, Bunn—er... Tracy..." Tracy's ex, Chucky Denning, flashed a worried look my way, but I just smiled and shook my head.

John Knox and his wife, Marta, stopped by to say hello. John had gotten himself a suit that actually fit, which was nice, but that wasn't the big news of the night. Marta, looking far healthier and happier than she had when I'd last seen her, patted the still small swell of her belly and beamed with pride. Tracy's eyes welled up and she threw her arms around the couple.

I glanced away and spotted Benny Hong a few feet away. I touched Tracy's shoulder and she turned.

"Trace, you remember Mr. Hong, don't you?"

She looked at Benny, back up at me, and said, "Um..?"

Benny extended his hand. Tracy took it. Benny was surprisingly gentle, thankfully.

It was Benny I'd gone to meet at Din Ho (back when I was being coy). Hong was a bit shorter than Tracy (she was in heels, though), but much *wider*, and none of it was fat. It was easy to forget his somewhat diminutive stature because the man seemed to be carved out of one hundred percent intimidation. His hair was longer now than it had been, and fell just over the collar of his dress shirt. He was, for once, clean-shaven, but far from making him look more presentable, it highlighted the hard lines of his face and a thin scar that ran from the corner of one eye down to his jaw line. And though he'd taken Tracy's hand very gently, his eyes – one whitish blue and the other a brown so deep as to appear black – only knew how to glare, apparently.

Weirdly, Tracy didn't appear intimidated at all. Recognition lit her features and she said, "Oh my gosh! You're the guy who—"

She looked at me and winced.

So, yeah. It's a long story, but I fought Benny once upon a not-that-long-ago. It was a tournament, and the thing everyone seems to remember from the damned thing is that Hong nailed me in the groin with a kick so powerful that my great-great grandfather probably felt it. Nobody remembers that I got him back, it seems, or that I *won* that fight. But I did. So there.

As an aside, apparently it's not that long of a story.

"Yeah," I said. "Tracy, I wanted you to meet Mr. Hong because he's going to be working with us soon."

Tracy smiled, but the arched eyebrow remained. "Oh?"

"Yes. Mr. Hong has agreed to be our nanny."

The smile slipped. "...What?"

"I assure you, Ms. Sandoval, I am very good with children," Benny said. I was on Benny's side – I'd hired him, after all – but even I had to admit that it wasn't totally clear, here, if he meant caring for them... or cooking them.

And I could tell that Tracy was thinking the same thing.

She turned to me and stared.

"Maybe nanny is too strong of a word... I hired Mr. Hong because I wanted to make sure that you had help around the house... and stuff. He's great, seriously. He cooks, he cleans..."

"I even do windows," Benny grunted.

I jabbed a thumb in his direction and grinned at Tracy. "See? How great is that?"

Tracy looked past me, caught the sight of a waiter, and said, "I think I would like a drink, Randall."

"That sounds like a great idea," I said, following her. I glanced back at Benny, who shrugged. I gave him a thumbs up and went back to following Tracy.

Tracy snagged a glass of champagne off the waiter's tray and turned on me. "What is this, Randall? I mean, don't get me wrong, I love it. It's beautiful here, and it's great to see everyone, and all that... but what the hell are you doing? I mean... the stuff earlier with the lawyer... and all of this... If you're trying to make me feel like a fairy princess or something, it's working, but it also makes me wonder... *What. Did. You. Do?*"

I frowned. The waiter offered me a glass, so I took it, drained it, and coughed. Champagne has never really been my thing. I always thought it was a bit like drinking fizzy perfume or something.

"What's that supposed to mean?" I said.

Tracy sighed. "It means that I *know* you. And I know when you're up to something. And whenever you fuck up, you make some grand gesture or whatever to get back in my good graces. So what is it this time? What did you do?"

It was suddenly very quiet, as the music had ended and everyone turned toward us. I cast a pleading look at Chucky, hoping he would hurry up and throw on a song, but instead he just gave me a two-fingered devil horn heavy metal salute.

I reached into my pocket and looked back at the girl of my dreams. She of the purple hair and the tattoos, bearer of the greatest pair of legs ever to grace the earth. That was all people usually saw, and, hey, I'd be lying if I said it wasn't what attracted me to her at first. But for those lucky enough to get to know her, they would see her beautiful mind, her kindness and compassion, her devotion. And sure, there were plenty of people who didn't get it. There always would be. For some, Tracy would always be my mid-life crisis piece of ass and nothing more. They never really saw her. On the other hand, some would always say I was the guy who hurt her, who put her in danger and almost got her killed on multiple occasions. I'd like to think that they don't see me. Sure, it's true that we almost killed each other once, but it's also true that I saved her once. And she saves me every single day.

"You're right," I said, taking her hand. "but, this time at least, I can say with certainty. I didn't fuck up."

She looked down as I slipped the ring onto her finger and I heard her gasp a little. By the time she looked back at me, I was kneeling in front of her. Tears spilled from her eyes.

"Tracy Ann Sandoval—"

She blurted out a, "YES."

The assembled crowd of loved ones applauded. Some laughed. I waited until the noise died down and said, "Could I finish, please?"

Tracy bit her lip, nodded, and wiped her eyes.

I took a deep breath, waited for everyone to settle once more, and said, "Tracy, will you—"

"Yes," she said, dropping to her knees and cupping my face in her hands. "Yes."

"—marry—"

She kissed me hard. I'd like to say that it was one of those beautiful storybook kisses, but it wasn't. Our teeth clanked together and my bottom lip got clipped. What I can tell you is that I didn't care. My teeth hurt and I tasted blood in my mouth, but I just didn't care.

"*Yes,*" she whispered.

"—me?" I said.

Her eyes met mine and she nodded vigorously. Then she grinned and kissed me again, softer.

I wouldn't have known if people applauded again, or if they booed. I couldn't tell you what song played to celebrate her answer or if there was only silence. The rest of the world fell away for that moment, and there was only the two of us. For that minute or so, all was right with the world.

There was dinner, and dancing, and drinking (well, other people drank. I had a refreshing cranberry juice, which only slightly sucked my will to live), and I'd like to think a good time was had by all. I had a few minor panic attacks whenever I lost track of my kid, but she was nearly always with her grandmother, so I was able to manage my freak outs pretty effectively.

Other than that, the only other awkward moment of the evening happened toward the end of the night. All attendees were given little gift bags on their way out, with the expectation that they would probably wait to open them until they got home. Leave it to Tracy's dad to go rummaging while his wife took one last hit of the super addictive drug that is holding my tiny munchkin daughter.

"…What..? What is this? Is this real?" Lawrence Sandoval said, holding up one of the golden tickets I had printed for the event. I had been sitting with Tony and Daniel, but I quickly excused myself and tried to contain things as much as possible. Without actually running, shoving waiters out of the way, or leaping over tables, I made my way over to him as fast as I could and said, "Hey… Why don't we talk about this tomorrow, okay? All the details are in the bag, and you can read up on it or whatever…"

But it was too late. Another guest, Tracy's friend Bernadette (a ridiculously pretty, Amazonian redhead) must have heard Lawrence and, naturally, decided to check out her gift bag as well. "Oh my god…" I heard her say. Rather loudly.

And that was that.

In seemingly less than a minute, everybody was rushing to check their bags. Since the rest of the night had gone so well it wasn't like I was an enormous failure or anything, I just hadn't counted on the average human's excitement at getting stuff.

So, yeah, it got a little weird.

I hadn't discussed any of this with Tracy, so, with everyone digging into their bags and finding their golden tickets (a design I deliberately cribbed off one of Tracy's favorite movies, *Willy Wonka and the Chocolate Factory)*, the bride was the last person at the party to know when and where she was getting married.

The when: In twelve weeks.

The where: Hong Kong.

When I saw that the news filtered down to her, I smiled sheepishly and said, "Surprise!"

***

Tracy had stockpiled milk back at her place, and her parents graciously agreed to take Faith and watch her for awhile so we could visit with some of our friends, namely Tony and Daniel and the Knoxes. The rest of Tracy's family had cleared out and most of her friends were gone, too, by this point. Tracy had maybe two glasses of champagne but, combined with lack of sleep, she was fairly trashed. She'd fallen asleep leaning against me, and we all pretended to listen to John Knox's latest police story.

I say pretended because there was significant tension coming from Tony's side of the table. Daniel slumped in his wheelchair and stared at his feet, and this is what he'd done most of the night. I'm pretty sure Knox started his story just to break the silence, but his babbling skills were nowhere near as good as mine, so he was starting to falter. Knox was in the middle of a sentence when, without warning, Daniel backed his chair up and started to wheel himself away. Tony immediately stood and, taking the handles on the back of the chair, asked Daniel where he needed to go.

Daniel mumbled an answer, which I took to mean that he had to use the restroom and didn't particularly want to announce that to the whole room. My hunch was confirmed a moment later when Daniel yelled, "I can do it *myself*."

Tony backed away and, as Daniel made his way to the back, returned to the table.

"I'm sorry," he said, quietly. "I think it may be time for us to leave."

"Why don't you guys come by the shop tomorrow around

noon?" I said.

Tony sighed and said, "I'll try. We'll have to see how he's feeling tomorrow morning."

The poor guy looked ill. He, too, had lost some weight, and the bags under his eyes told me I wasn't the only one having trouble sleeping.

I gave him a sympathetic smile.

"Okay," I said, "but do try. Tell him he needs to see the doctor."

***

By the time we got to Tracy's apartment, everyone was asleep. Tracy tried to wake up her dad, but he said they were fine sleeping on the couches. I have to say, if you have to sleep on the couch (as I have many a time), Tracy's couches can't be beat.

We crept down the hall to Faith's room and peeked in at her. She was asleep in her usual position: on her back, with her arms clasped behind her head. It looked a bit weird for such a small baby to sleep like a retiree in a hammock, but we frequently knew when she was tired because her hands would start to drift upward, seemingly of their own accord, into the position. As we watched, Faith sucked at her bottom lip rhythmically and, finding no milk there, let out a quiet sigh.

I felt eyes on me and looked over to see Tito sprawled out across Faith's changing table, an indignant look upon his wrinkled face, as if we had no business being there.

"Uh oh. Did Grampy and Grammy accidentally let wittle bonito Tito into the bebbe's room?" Tracy said in a low, sing-songy whisper. She scooped up Tito and swept him to her breast. She wasn't immediately shredded by whirling claws of death, which was weird considering he once tried to trip me down a flight of stairs for just scolding him.

"Let's get you to bed, Mister," Tracy said. She turned on the ball of one foot and headed out, the yellow eyes of her pet scrotum demon glaring mockingly over her shoulder at me.

I took a deep breath, fished my keys from my pocket, and said, "I guess I'll see you tomorrow afternoon?"

Tracy stopped, turned very slightly, and in the dim light of the hall I could still make out her smile. "I was talking to you... *Mister*."

"W-Wh-huh?"

Smooth as silk, per usual. As Tracy would say, I win at all the things.

Tracy crooked her finger and I felt like one of those old cartoon guys, levitating along after the beckoning girl, with toes barely dragging along the floor. As a result, I'm not sure how we got to her bedroom, but there we were.

"Your parents are still here," I said. "They're, like, twenty feet away."

"So lock the door. And I promise to be quiet," she said, putting Tito down on the dresser. He made a small squawking sound. Then, with a minor flick of her fingers to unfasten some hidden button or zipper, she sent her dress cascading to the floor, unveiling what seemed to my eyes like miles of intoxicatingly pale, silky flesh clad only in a deep violet and black lace bra and panties.

"Can *you* promise to be quiet, Randall?" she said.

It is possible that I may have, upon seeing her mostly unclothed body for the first time in a year, made a sound not unlike that of the last lingering breath of a slowly dying wildebeest. Tracy swears this is the case. In the interest of full disclosure, I have no idea what I was or wasn't doing. Or, in fairness, the sound of a slowly dying wildebeest. But I was definitely staring. And possibly calculating the amount of Gatorade I was going to need.

Electrolytes.

The struggle is real.

Whatever sound I was allegedly making, Tracy cut it short by deftly and securely applying her mouth to mine. With her body pressed against me and my hands on her warm skin, the rest of the world went away again. I truly cannot overstate this. I completely forgot about Tracy's parents in the next room. I forgot about all my aches and pains. I stopped worrying about Faith and Daniel and Beatrix. All I knew was her sly smile in the darkness, the heat of her breath, the scent of her skin, warm vanilla and a hint of coconut, the feel of her body. Everything else went away.

How were we on the bed?

Total mystery.

Where the hell had my pants gone?

No idea.

But then Tracy shrugged out of her bra and I completely forgot whatever else I was thinking about.

Here's the thing, though. From the very beginning, the two of us have always been a bit intense. I tend to think of myself as a somewhat reserved individual when it comes to most things. Usually. Tracy is one of the few exceptions. For instance, once, when we first started dating, we had planned to go to the zoo. Tracy came to my place and, five minutes after she arrived, a freak apocalyptic thunderstorm (well, in Missouri they just call that "weather") swept in, complete with dark greenish skies and *sideways* sheets of rain. Clearly the zoo was out. Instead, Tracy asked me to teach her to play Mah Jong.

The actual game, not that ridiculous computer thing where you just match tiles.

I was in the middle of explaining to her about Pungs, Kongs, and Chows when I looked up in time to see her tuck a strand of hair behind her ear. Her eyes met mine for a brief second before she looked back down at her tiles. Fast forward an hour, and there's a toppled card table, underwear hanging from the ceiling fan, and a random pattern of tile-shaped bruises in my back.

And it's not like that was the only time.

We have always had a very... *physical*... relationship. Which is part of what has made the past year so tough. It's not the sex, however great that is (and, not to brag, but it really is pretty great). It's the touch. The closeness. *The trust.*

So here we were, seemingly back to the good old days. I could feel her heart pounding hard next to mine, hear her breath quickening and her muscles tensing beneath me. Only by pulling back, seeing her face lit by moonlight, did I realize that these cues did not mean what I thought they meant.

I eased back from her and offered her my hands.

"Just... Have to... Breathe... Just for a minute. I'm so sorry," she panted, sitting up and sliding back to lean against the headboard.

"What can I do? Let me help. Please?" I said. I felt lost. The old hurt, the regret, twisted in my gut, reminding me.

I did this.

And I could never take it back and it was never going away.

My eyes went to her ankle, to the six inch scar from a compound break that had taken two different surgeries to fix. It was the only physical scar from the attack, but it was enough. The worst of the damage couldn't be seen, but we could feel it every time we were together. The closeness we had was gone. The trust was history.

Tracy fumbled for something from the nightstand. I saw a bottle of pills fall to the floor and quickly retrieved them. I got her a glass of water from her bathroom. She swallowed a handful of pills, drained the glass of water, and slumped, holding her face in her hands.

"I'm so sorry, Randall."

"It's okay," I said.

"No, it's not."

"Fair enough," I said. "It's not okay. It sucks. I hate it. But it's not your fault."

"It's my stupid brain."

"It's your brilliant brain trying to protect you."

Tracy looked up at me. Her mascara was smudged by tears and her nose was red.

"I know you won't hurt me. I *know* it. I have to tell myself a hundred times a day, but I *know* that's the truth. What happened wasn't your fault any more than it was mine, but I don't know how to turn off that part of my brain. I want this so bad, Randall. I want us to be us."

I took a deep breath and sat back on the bed.

"It was here. Right here," I said.

She nodded.

She had crawled into the bedroom, her ankle shattered, and tried to hide from me. In my Jade-fueled fury, I'd taken great joy in dragging her back to me by her broken ankle. And I punched her and kicked her and tried to strangle her.

Right where we sat.

Right here.

Tracy had her knees pulled to her chest. I reached out, slowly, and put my hand on her foot.

"I am so sorry, Tracy."

She sniffled and nodded.

"I want us to be us, too," I said.

Very slowly, very gently, I took her foot in my hands and straightened her leg, bringing my lips to her instep. I moved a few inches and kissed the scar on the outer edge of her ankle. She giggled softly.

"Babe, I have to tell you, if you've decided to pick this moment to tell me about some weird new fetish... this is super awkward timing."

I flashed a playful frown at her and brought my lips to her shin, then to the inside of her calf. I watched her the entire time, her expression changing from worry to curiosity to amusement. I worked my way up to just above her knees when she said, "Stop."

I froze.

"Hm," she said, tapping her lip with a perfectly manicured fingernail. "Or maybe don't."

So I continued. A few minutes later, she said, "Stop."

I froze again.

She leaned back on the bed, propping herself up on her elbows. She looked down at me now, playfully biting her lip, and said, "How interesting."

"What is?" I said.

"Apparently... Well, my brain has, so far, been very, very quiet."

"That *is* interesting," I said.

"Lay back and be still," she said.

I did.

Mimicking me, Tracy kissed the ugly scar on the palm of my hand and moved down to the small pinkish crater in my stomach. I found myself hoping that we weren't having some kind of weird scar-kissing competition because a) I'd win, b) It would take hours for her to cover the roadmap of horror, courage, and outright stupidity that was etched into my body, and c) Ew.

But that wasn't what happened. And it wasn't some ultra-kinky dominatrix stuff that went down, either, if that's what you're thinking. No, what happened, over the course of many hours, was a slow and gentle reacquainting, a testing and a rebuilding of trust. It may not have been what the impatient animal of my brain wanted, but it was what she needed.

When the first rays of sun peeked over the horizon and, with
laser focus, stabbed directly into my eyes, I allowed myself a
minute of agitation before remembering that I was entwined with a
very lovely, very naked woman. Things could be – and had been –
worse.

Way worse.

I didn't want to disturb Tracy or anything, but the beam of sun
was intense enough to give me a headache even through closed
eyelids so I carefully pulled away from her and sat up, moving
away from the solar death ray. The apartment was quiet, and the
city below seemed to be struggling to get moving as well.

I threw on some clothes, if 'threw' meant to slowly, creakily
dress in such a way as to not pull a muscle or fall over and crack
my skull on something. Tito rammed into my leg and wound
himself between my feet, rubbing his weird, wrinkly body along
my ankles. I bent slowly and gave him a scratch behind his ears.
He seemed genuinely happy to see me, as if he were giving me the
cat equivalent of a high five for managing to spend the night.

Then he flipped onto his back, clutching my arm, and kicked the
shit out of my hand with his evil little demon claws.

What an asshole.

Once I'd stopped the bleeding, I grabbed some clean clothes
from my little corner of Tracy's closet and took a quick shower. At
least, I thought it had been a quick shower.

When I emerged from the bathroom, everyone was awake.
Tracy was making pancakes for her parents, who sat around
Tracy's small table, drinking coffee. Genevieve was holding Faith,
who spotted me immediately and yelled out 'Gah!' at my
approach.

Lawrence said, "No, Faith, that's 'Da,' not 'Gah.'"

She replied, "Ta! Taaaaaaplllblblblblblblblb!"

"Good point," I said.

***

After a long and mostly awkward "family" breakfast, Tracy's
parents planned to take her and Faith shopping. Again. Trace said

she might try to divert them off to the zoo instead (since we really didn't need anything) and asked me to come, but I politely declined. Then I gave her one of my credit cards and said that her parents were not to spend a dime. This was both the right thing to do and a way to be contrary, dominant, and kind of an asshole, so I felt pretty good about it.

While they went to the zoo, I went back to my place. Or what used to be my place. It had been taken over by a crotchety, ancient Chinese man, supposedly only for a few weeks… but I didn't see anything to indicate that he planned to move back to his place any time soon. I unlocked my door and walked in to find him sitting stiffly on my couch, intently watching a fishing show on television.

"Where were you last night?" I said.

"Odd. You do not look like my father, and he was the last person to demand my whereabouts."

"Did you forget? Our engagement dinner?"

"Did *you* forget? I do not drive."

"I sent Knox to pick you up. He said you didn't answer the door."

Cheng looked at me in surprise. "Why would I answer the door for a stranger?"

I stared back at him. "Knox isn't a stranger. And you're not an eight year old girl."

"…Knox… Was he the policeman?"

"Yes. You know him."

Cheng sniffed and said, "I do not open the door for policemen." I sighed.

"Well, you really missed out. It was a beautiful evening, and both Tracy and I wanted you there, but, clearly, sitting in your pajamas and watching reality television is more important."

Cheng picked up the remote control. As he flipped channels he said, "Better for you. The young do not want to be reminded of the old. Last thing new couple wants to see is old, bitter widow."

I walked over to the couch and sat down next to him. "Hey," I said. "Are you okay?"

"Sure, sure. No problem."

"If you need to talk…" I started.

Cheng snorted. "Great American answer for everything? Let out the feelings? Ha. If this works so well, why does America have so many problems, eh? Seem to me a way for nosey people to make money being nosey. If you must know, I am fine. My life is simple, and the life of a simple man is filled with pleasure. I have, for instance, learned much about the fishing of the big-mouth American fish this morning. I have dined on a bowl of that foul porridge made from oats which you people seem to love, and I have had a satisfying bowel movement. With this much activity, it is possible I shall need to nap soon. I will, however, wait until you are finished playing the concerned student, for it would be rude to do otherwise."

I opened my mouth to say something but immediately forgot what that would have been. So I closed my mouth. Then I opened it again, the perfect comeback springing to mind, for once, at the perfect time. Almost, anyway. Then I closed my mouth again because whatever I would have said would not have been the sort of thing anyone should say to one of their elders, even if that elder happened to persist in being a major dickhead at least some of the time. So I took a second, hoping to temper my thoughts, to soften them somehow into something a bit kinder and gentler, something that Cheng could accept and appreciate without feeling hurt.

In the meantime, the old bastard said, "I see now why your Tai Chi suffers so. You clearly put all your time and effort into this fish impersonation which, while impressive, does not seem very practical."

"Y'know what? Screw you. I don't know what the hell your problem is and, yeah, to be honest I don't really care right now. I know you're my teacher and I know that I owe you so much that I'll never be able to repay you and I know that you're an old man who's had a rough life and all of that, but I also know that you live in my apartment and you eat my food and drink all the soda and all I'm asking, literally all I am asking of you, is to make an attempt to not be a raging asshole to me every minute. Is that a crazy expectation? I don't think so. What do you think?"

Cheng's face folded into an unreadable mass of wrinkles.

I looked down at the gift bag in my hands. I tossed it onto the couch and said, "Here. If you can be bothered, Tracy and I would like to fly you to Hong Kong for our wedding. Because yes, we love you and we want you there. You may think we don't, but it's not really up to you, you grumpy old fuck."

He looked up at me slowly, eyes wide and uncomprehending, but he said nothing. I let out something that was somewhere between a sigh and a growl and went to my bedroom. I took another quick shower and changed into some comfortable clothes before emerging back into the living room. Cheng was standing now, pacing in slow motion, and the contents of the gift bag were strewn across the couch. He held the golden ticket in his hands and stared at it as he paced.

"What?" I said.

He didn't look up at me when he said, "I have never been back. Not since…"

Cheng had lost his kids, a son and a daughter, back during the Cultural Revolution. Seeing his homeland go mad, he and his wife had managed to escape the Red Guard by sneaking into Hong Kong in the middle of the night. That had been in 1974. And while the revolution ended in 1976, Cheng's attachment to his home had been permanently broken.

"I know," I said. "Maybe it's time to give it a chance?"

He looked up at me then, eyes unreadable. "You and young Tracy wish for me to go?"

I nodded. We did. He was like a father to me. A foul-mouthed, insulting, elitist father, but still… there was a quality to the man that made it tough to be around him while simultaneously daring you not to love him.

He slipped the ticket into his pocket and said, "Then I will go."

Without another word, he shuffled off to the bathroom.

And that was that.

***

The first day with Daniel could have gone better.

I left Cheng to his television shows and went down to the shop in time to see Tony and Daniel park. Fifteen minutes later, I watched them leave again. And in the brief minutes between arrival and departure, a whole lot of awkwardness, pain, and general existential malaise.

It was clear that Daniel didn't want to be there. That Tony had pushed him to come. That, for whatever reason, he didn't want anything to do with me at all. I got enough of that sort of thing from the vast majority of planet earth, and I didn't really expect to get it from someone I considered a friend.

On their way out the door, Tony flashed a look of apology and said, he'd call me later.

I went to the back room, grabbed a bottle of Coke from the fridge, and stared at the notes I'd taken during our brief and thoroughly shitty session. Daniel had given me a chance to examine him a bit, taking his pulses, checking his tongue, poking around on his legs, that sort of thing. The pulse readings were all pretty decent… a little sluggish, maybe, but he was on medication and dealing with depression, so I figured that wasn't out of the ordinary. The main thing I noticed while checking his tongue was that the bastard had a perfect set of teeth. I mean flawless. Just thinking about it, I wanted to dump my Coke down the drain and run upstairs to floss for like an hour and a half.

The legs were a different story. During the fight with Mark Van Allen, Daniel had taken a hell of a beating, culminating in spectacularly ugly compound tibial-fibular fractures in both legs and bad hyperextension of both knees. His lower body was held together with enough hardware to open a Home Depot, and, according to Daniel, he could feel it. Changes in the weather, fluctuations in humidity, even minute physical movements transformed those innocent bits of modern medical technology into white hot shrapnel.

The pain, he said, was almost constant. At best, the dull roar of it drained his daily life of its color and flavor. At its worst, the world grew teeth; inescapable razors whose bite kept him from sleep. On those days, even breathing hurt.

After the phone call that night from Tony, I got him to agree to bring Daniel back the next day. The rest was a bit harder, but he eventually agreed to that, too.

When Tony came that next day, just as we'd discussed, he wheeled Daniel into the shop and, without a word, left. Daniel protested, but I'd told Tony that would happen.

I wheeled him within four feet of the treatment table. "Okay, here you go. Hop up on the table and we'll get started."

Daniel just glared at me.

"What?" I said.

"I can't," he said.

"I'll give you a hand," I said. I put a hand on his shoulder, ready to support him, but he slapped it away. Rather vigorously, I might add.

I shook my hand and muttered a curse under my breath before saying, "Look, the table's right there. I can't work on you from the chair…"

"I never said I wanted you to. I want to go back to the hotel."

"That wasn't the deal. Tony asked me to help get you back on your feet—"

"Take me back to the hotel. Now."

I frowned.

"Or what?" I said.

"What?"

I leaned back against the treatment table and crossed my arms. It is true that the table started to roll away and I had to stand up quickly to avoid losing my balance, but that isn't really relevant so let's just forget it.

"I said, 'Or what?' What do you suppose you're going to do if I *don't* take you back?"

Daniel narrowed his eyes.

"I'll leave. I'll call a cab."

"Really? You'll leave? How? You think you're going to just roll on out of here? I will knock your ass right out of that chair, gimpy."

Daniel just stared at me. He may have sputtered slightly.

"It seems to me that you've been getting by, these last few months, by proclaiming yourself to be King of the Assholes. I'm here to tell you that you're not. As long as I'm around, you're not even part of the Asshole royal family. At best, you're like a douchey squire."

Daniel backed his chair up about an inch before I planted a foot on his right wheel.

"Do you think I'm kidding?" I said.

He shoved my foot off the wheel and spun toward the door. I sighed, hoping that things wouldn't actually go this way. But, having spent a lot of time reading parenting books and realizing just how important it is to follow through on the things one says, I took a step forward, and, without malice, toppled Daniel's wheelchair, spilling him face first onto the carpet.

It was not one of my prouder moments.

"You son of a bitch!"

And yes, I deserved that. Everything would've gone to crap, though, if I'd immediately turned apologetic, so instead I doubled down on my assholery.

"I told you, didn't I?"

"I'll fucking kill you!"

He sounded sincere, but the kick he threw at my shin lacked both strength and any sort of technique.

I told him so.

He cursed some more.

I leaned over and cuffed him across the top of the head.

Like magic, I found myself face to seething, hate-filled face with one of the most dangerous men I'd ever met in my life.

I told him that, too.

It took him off his guard a bit.

"What?" he said.

"I said, 'Welcome back.' I don't know who that other guy was, but he was a sad, weak sack of flatulence. This guy here? I mean, sure, he could stand to eat a quarter pounder or two, but I recognize the icy cold stare of a merciless killing machine and, frankly, it fills my heart with joy. By the way, before you punch my head clean off my shoulders, you might want to notice what you're doing."

Daniel released the vice grip hold he had on the front of my shirt and looked down to see himself standing, supported only by the fiery rage of a thousand supernovas. Immediately, his legs began to shake violently.

I put an arm around his shoulders and said, "Too late, y'big faker. C'mon, let's get you to the table."

He made it, barely. Sweat streamed down a grimacing face turned ashen from strain. I helped him recline and, while he tried to catch his breath, I hit acupressure points on the backs of both calves to keep his muscles from cramping.

"You... really are... an asshole..." Daniel said.

I tore open a packet of needles with my teeth and said, "Hail to the king, baby."

***

That first day, Daniel walked maybe six steps.

Three days later, he walked from the front door of the shop to the table. And while the physical progress should've been heartening, Daniel's mental state remained low and unpredictable. He no longer fought coming to the shop, though, or getting acupuncture, so that was something.

And since he could stand for short periods, we began practicing qigong together. While I wasn't standing on two broken legs, it still sucked. Something so simple shouldn't be so painful, but it was. The only sure way out of it was to keep going, through the pain, through the doubt, and out the other side.

By the end of the first week, he was able to stand for one minute.

Sixty whole seconds.

Afterward we celebrated with pizza.

I would've loved to have added a six pack to that, but with Daniel's meds and my… attempting to *not* add six packs to everything, we settled for a locally made soda that was perfectly fine, for soda, but which was a terrible substitute for beer.

When Tony came to pick Daniel up that day, I asked how long they planned to stay.

Tony shrugged and said, "I guess that depends."

He looked at Daniel. Daniel didn't meet his gaze, didn't look at anyone, really, but said, "I want to stay longer."

Tony put a hand on his shoulder and squeezed. He looked up at me and nodded.

***

"So I took my folks to get their passports renewed."

I was watching Faith. She was "sitting" in a sort of strangely-crafted recumbent seat for babies. Tito was attempting to sleep on her lap, but she kept patting him on the head. Vigorously. He looked super pissed, but he took it. Every now and then his eyes would meet mine and I'd hear a rasping sound that I realized was the devilcat version of a sigh.

"Cool," I said, turning back to Tracy. "Everything go okay?"

"I think so, yeah. How are things going with Daniel?"

I grabbed the cardboard container of rice and scooped some onto my plate next to an embarrassing pile of Chongqing chicken. We were currently having a carpet picnic in the middle of my living room. Cheng had been gone for the afternoon and the place was weirdly quiet without him.

I shrugged and tossed the closed container back onto the carpet.

"Slowly," I said. "I mean, not really… He's doing really well… but it still feels slow to me. Every time I think we've moved forward he comes in and it's like he's regressed… I don't know."

Tracy watched me as I spoke and popped a cube of Mapo Doufu in her mouth. "Well," she said after a sip of soda, "you just have to be patient. He's been through a lot."

"Yeah."

I hadn't meant that one word to come out in the most bitter and shitty way possible, but it had. A single syllable which came to mean, "He should really take a number because everyone – including our baby – has been through a lot. Hell, *I've* been through a lot, too, y'know… and you don't hear me bitching and moaning about it, do you? And maybe I don't have any more patience. What then?"

Tracy set her plate on the carpet and, in a move that came off as both tender and somehow kittenish, rose up onto her knees and crawled over to kiss me lightly on the lips. It was probably just the Sichuan peppercorn content of the Mapo Doufu, but I found that my lips went numb within seconds of the kiss.

She put a cool palm against my cheek and gazed into my eyes so intently that it was difficult, uncomfortable somehow, to maintain the contact.

"You know… You can't save everybody."

I sat, listening to the silence punctuated every few seconds by the sound of a moist baby palm against the velveteen head of a very perturbed Sphinx.

"What is *that* supposed to mean?"

"It means that you're surrounded by all these poor little wounded birds, and you've convinced yourself that everything that ever happened to anyone you know is all your fault, so you're determined to save everyone... and sooner or later, you're just going to have to let it all go."

I stared at her.

"You know better than most people, Randall, that there are bad people in the world. Their job is to hate and to destroy. It's kind of their jam. So you can't think that it's your fault if bad people do bad things. The thing with me and with Daniel... none of it is your fault."

I said, "No, Daniel–"

"Would've been there anyway. You guys told me that he was in that tournament to represent Tony's interests. He wasn't there for you. At all. You kept that guy from killing Daniel, and that's all. And whatever Daniel's problems are now – and I hope to God that he gets over them – they are not your fault. He's not your obligation. You have to let that weight go, baby."

"I almost killed you."

Tracy shook her head and smiled. "No, McGarrity almost killed me. He could've used a gun or a knife or a bomb, but instead he decided to use a very sexy, occasionally hilarious, frequently-far-too-emo-for-his-own-good acupuncturist. And while that whole incident was a truckload of bad times, y'know what? He *failed*. And for all my issues, Randall, I'm still here. I'm here and Faith is here and we're a family. And McGarrity? Who even knows where that loser is, but wherever he is I know that he's probably plotting to ruin someone else's day. I also know that he's a miserable sack of shit, and he'll always be a miserable sack of shit and that makes me feel a little bit bad for him. He'll never have *this*. He'll never have what we have, right here, right now. Because that's the thing with the bad people, Randall: that's their jam, too. If they were happy and well-adjusted people, they wouldn't spend so much time and energy trying to fuck up everything for everyone else."

She smiled, and her dark eyes were so sincere, so sweet. Far from the desired effect, Tracy's little speech made me feel terrible.

I knew, looking into those eyes, that I was not a good person.

I would never be a good person.

"Hong Kong," I said. "McGarrity's in Hong Kong."

Tracy's smile faded.

"You're right, Trace. He's one of the bad people, one of the worst, and he knows us. He's out there, and I won't sleep at night until I know that he isn't anymore."

Tears filled her eyes.

"And the wedding? It was all... what? Part of some scheme?"

I shook my head.

"No. No scheme. Just... complimentary interests."

"...Wow."

She stood up and wiped at her eyes before bending to scoop a grateful Tito off Faith's lap and into his cat carrier. Faith began to cry.

"You have to understand," I said.

"No, I don't."

"Look, I have people keeping tabs on him. I wanted to keep everyone together, to keep everyone safe. And the best wedding present I could think of was to give you and Faith – and myself – a lifetime of peace. I don't want to spend every day looking over my shoulder. I don't want to wonder, every time the phone rings, if something has happened to one of you."

"Randall, it's over."

"*It* isn't *over until he is no longer a threat.*"

It occurred to me that maybe that wasn't what she meant, but I didn't want to accept that.

I'm not sure I could've accepted that.

She picked up Faith and bounced her a little to soothe her. It was not terribly effective.

"Trace... I am sorry. I know how it all looks, but I never did any of this to hurt you. I just..."

She wasn't paying attention. She was leaving. Just like that.

"I can't lose you," I said. "I can't lose Faith. And if you want to know why I do the stupid things I do, that's why. Because that's what I think of when you're not around. That's what wakes me up at night. And I can't face that. I can't do it, not again."

She turned and I thought I saw a faint flicker of sympathy for the briefest second.

"...I'll call you," she said.

Then they were gone.

***

"Ow!"

"Well, stop fucking standing that way. If you straighten your leg again, you will get hit again. You'll learn sooner or later. "

Daniel grimaced and sank into his stance.

It wasn't much. It wasn't like I was asking him to do a full horse stance or anything, I just wanted him to start to sink a bit. And when he tried to rise up, it's true... I did whack him on a pressure point on the side of the thigh with a rattan escrima stick. Still, he was being a bit of a baby about the whole thing. It's just that the lower stances were stronger, and I was feeling particularly impatient that day.

Tracy hadn't called yet.

"What the hell is your problem today?" he said.

Tracy hadn't called yet.

"Nothing. I'm just not loving your attitude today."

Daniel glared at me. "I don't have an attitude. You've just been a prick all morning. When you did the needles earlier I thought you were trying to engrave on the bone or something..."

"Right. Because you're an expert in acupuncture. Focus. You're coming up from your stance again."

"Because it feels like my leg is going to break."

"Well, it's not. Your bones are healed. You're just being a whiny bitch."

"Fuck you."

I raised an eyebrow and said, "Tony wouldn't appreciate that, and it wouldn't improve your form any."

His legs were shaking violently. He clenched his jaw hard enough to powder teeth and grunted, "I hate you."

"Yeah, well... lot of that going around. Come on up."

Instead of standing up, though, he fell onto his ass.

And that, naturally, is when Tony decided to walk in. He was at Daniel's side in a moment. "Jesus. Are you okay?"

Daniel nodded. Then they both looked at me.

"What?" I said.

"Maybe you could go a little easier?" Tony said.

I took a deep breath and let it out slowly. It didn't help.

"Look, whatever you might think, this stuff isn't supposed to be easy. I never said it would be easy. All I said was that it would work. In the meantime, though, he has to work his ass off. And guess what? It's going to hurt, and it's going to suck every single second that he's doing it, but when he's able to walk across a room without a cane, he'll thank me."

Tony didn't say anything. He looked back at Daniel, put an arm around him, and helped him back to his feet. Daniel's legs began to shake almost immediately and he had to sit again. The muscles in his face were iron cables straining against sweat-slicked ashen skin.

My intention wasn't to break him down. I didn't think I'd been that hard on him. The weakness, though, the way *everything* was hard for him... I'm not sure why, but it made me so angry. It just wasn't *him.*

While Tony comforted Daniel, I grabbed a half-full jar of Cheng's very potent dit da jow liniment from the back room. Now that I was walking around, I realized that we *had* been hitting it pretty hard. The muscles in my lower back were a warm, pleasant sort of sore, but the muscles in my legs were demolished. The old wounds made themselves known, the new skin unpleasantly taut, still.

"Here," I said, and tossed the jar to Tony. "Rub this into the muscles. It'll help."

Daniel looked up at me, still pained. "I don't think... I'm sorry, but I don't think I can do anymore today."

"No. We're done for today," I said.

Daniel grinned with obvious relief and, I saw, more than a little embarrassment.

I felt a tightness in my chest, a sickening feeling.

"What about lunch? You guys want to grab lunch? It's on me."

They looked at me like I was insane. Lots of people looked at me that way, though, so it didn't hurt my feelings or anything.

"I'm drenched in sweat and I can hardly move," Daniel said slowly.

"So you go back to the hotel and shower and put on the ointment and we meet up in an hour or so."

After they'd agreed and Tony helped Daniel hobble out to the car, I called and left another message for Tracy. I knew that it didn't help anything to badger her when she was like this (and she'd been like this more than a few times, mostly because I'm frequently a gigantic fucking asshole) but I wanted to at least let her know about the lunch plans. She was usually pretty good about putting our personal crap (about what a gigantic fucking asshole I happen to be) on the back burner long enough to spend time with friends. I didn't have high hopes, but I made the call anyway.

I went upstairs and took a shower, letting the hot water slowly start to unlock the muscles that had already cramped up tightly. It's really not fair. You can spend twenty or thirty years learning something like Tai Chi but take a little time off (to get over being shot a few times) and it's like you're starting from scratch.

After getting dressed, I found Cheng meandering around the kitchen, slamming cupboards.

"Can I help you?" I said.

"Tea."

"…Oh… Are we out?"

He stopped where he was and turned to stare at me.

"Well, I'm supposed to meet Tony and Daniel for lunch at Szechuan Empire. I could pick some up on my way back?"

"You go to lunch now with those gay boys?"

I winced.

"You may call me old-fashioned, but–" "

I interrupted him. "Master, whatever you're about to say? Just don't."

He waved me off and continued, "–in my day, a person had lunch at noon. Not three o'clock. How do you expect to have an appetite for dinner? Also, in my day a respectful student would invite his beloved teacher… What? What are you looking at?"

"Well… it's just… the way you called them 'gay boys'…"

Cheng shrugged and said, "What? They're boys. They're gay. So?"

"Well, it's just… Hey. If you're so worried about a late lunch screwing up the appetite, why do you suddenly want to go?"

He looked at me blankly.

"Because. You. Are. Out. Of. Tea."

He slammed another cabinet and said, "I will get my jacket."

***

We were on our way to the restaurant, a tiny but excellent Sichuan place hidden in the middle of a strip mall, when Cheng said, "So, this Daniel…"

And that was that. He just left it hang there.

After waiting for at least a few minutes I said, "Yes?"

"What?"

"Was there more that you wanted to say? Like an actual complete sentence?"

"I said. I ask you what his problem is."

"No, you didn't. You–" I glanced over at him. One look at his face told me that it was pointless to argue. "He got hurt in that tournament, remember?"

"Still? So long ago!"

It wasn't *that* long ago, but I agreed with Cheng's general impatience.

"Well, he got really hurt."

Cheng grunted.

We drove on in silence for a few minutes, but eventually I couldn't take it.

"What?" I said.

"Hm?" he said.

"That grunt. What was that supposed to mean?"

Cheng sniffed loudly. "Not everything has meaning."

I sighed.

When we arrived at the restaurant, Cheng hurriedly unbuckled his seat belt and practically ran inside. In fact, the only time I'd seen him move faster was when people were shooting at us, but this was almost as fast. It was disconcerting, like watching a sloth sprint away from you. Though I was pretty stunned by the display, I happened to spot a black Chevy Cavalier with about a thousand bumper stickers all over the back. I hurried inside, too.

The place wasn't very big, and it looked relatively dumpy. White walls, sparsely adorned with yellowing newspaper clippings from local papers ("Best Oriental Food – 1989," and "St. Louis' Best Chop Suey," read a few of the cringe-worthy examples). A small shrine was set into one wall and a few mildly tacky wooden screens broke up the space here and there. The tables and chairs were cheap, with split seat cushions and chipped paint, but nobody came here for the atmosphere. Ms. Sun, a widow from Chengdu, was a bit much sometimes, but her food undeniably kicked much ass. Her son, the only other employee, approached and I told him I was meeting some people. He nodded and meandered off.

The place was pretty packed for a weekday afternoon, but I spotted Daniel and Tracy in the back near an amazingly tacky aquarium. They were facing away from me, and I didn't see Tony with them. As I made my way through the crowd, I saw Cheng near the kitchen window, talking animatedly (well, for him anyway) with Ms. Sun. I made a mental note to be as obnoxious and juvenile to him as possible later (think, "Cheeng and Suun, sittin' in a tree, k-i-s-s-i-n-g") but I was desperate to make things right again with Trace, so I hurried over.

As I got closer, I started to pick up on bits of their conversation.

"…be that anymore. He thinks he's being accepting, understanding, but it just makes it worse," Daniel said.

I decided to hang back a bit. There was a fake potted Ficus near one of the wooden screens, so I nonchalantly (as nonchalantly as one may) ducked behind the tree and hid. I realize that eavesdropping is terrible and rude and whatever. I've had far worse things on my conscience.

Tracy reached across the table and patted his hand. "I had a boyfriend back in college who was a singer in a kind of indie/soul band. They got to be kind of a big deal… he ended up cheating on me with probably every groupie between here and New York… anyway, before all that, he used to say that every night he had to take the time to 'give birth to' the guy he was going to be on stage. Like, it wasn't him. And it wasn't. He was this shy, kinda sweet…nerd, basically. But when he hit the stage, he turned, like, super suave and fuckin' tough. I mean, on that stage he was a total pimp. And sure, all that ended up pretty much imploding our relationship, but that explanation always stuck with me."

She took a sip of her iced tea and said, "*You* decide. That's what I took from it all. You create yourself, whoever you say you are, every day. So this is a setback, sure but you can get past it. You can rebuild yourself. You can be whatever you want to be… just be careful."

Daniel frowned and flashed a questioning look. Tracy fiddled with her straw and seemed guarded. She hesitated several times before finally speaking but once she began, her voice was strong.

"So..." Tracy said, "once upon a time there was this girl, okay? And she used to get picked on all the time in elementary school. Boys, girls, didn't matter. Everybody was mean to this poor kid. At night she would cry herself to sleep because she didn't know what to do, and she would beg her fairy godmother to do something, anything, to make the other kids like her. Do you know what happened?"

Daniel shook his head again.

"Puberty happened. And while some of the kids got caught with that awkward, neither-here-nor-there kind of look, the girl managed to finally catch a break. Like a girl in a fairy tale, one night the homely, shy kid went to bed and woke up a pretty, and suddenly rather curvy, young woman. The girl was a bit ashamed to admit it, but there was a teensy part of her, deep, deep down, that felt a bit excited by the way the boys started looking at her. So, against her parents' wishes, she started wearing makeup. And her skirts progressively got shorter. Shocker of shockers, boys started being even nicer to her. The girls, though, got even bitchier. So this totally made up, hypothetical girl started to hang out with the boys. She learned how boys talk and what boys do and, like an anthropologist studying a heretofore undiscovered tribe in deepest, darkest wherever, she assimilated. She learned to hang. And lo, this girl became that holiest of holy grails: The Cool Girlfriend.

"However much it hurt sometimes, however Not Cool she really was, this girl worked so, so hard at mastering every skill she needed. She was sexy. She was chill. She laughed at all the boys' jokes. She could talk football and play Xbox and fill her closet with all of Victoria's dirtiest secrets. She was golden. The world just... opened up.

"She met lots of super cool guys, this girl did. There were lots of parties and lots of good times, but it was all casual. Very chill. And that was cool because chill was what this girl was all about, right? It was all part of her training. So the boys came and the boys went, usually, and this ultra cool chick told herself that it was all good, because what point was there in getting tied down to anybody when there was so much awesome in the world? But then y'know what happened? The big ole turning point that totally jacked this chick's world?"

Daniel smiled faintly, patiently, and said, "She fell in love?"

Tracy said, "Huh? No, man!"

I frowned.

"I mean, yeah, she did. I guess. That was a different kind of jacked up, though. Because love was pretty chill, and like I said, chill is what this girl did. It barely smudged her Cool Girlfriend makeup. No, the thing that just demolished this girl's whole universe? The universe, in its infinite wisdom, decided to plant a tiny human inside her body."

Daniel frowned.

Me, too.

Tracy drank some more tea.

"Oh, don't get me wrong, this chick loves her spawn. This totally, totally fictional girl who I made up completely, but she has this problem: The Cool Girlfriend is never The Cool Wife and she is never, ever, ever, ever the Cool Mom. The Cool Girlfriend doesn't know how to mom it up. And it's not because she's spent thousands of dollars *and* hours transforming her body with art and needles and jewelry into the polar opposite of June Cleaver. This flower blooms at twilight and withers with the dawn. Oh, sure, she can make a bottle or change a diaper. Trained gorillas and even some boys can do that. What she wants to know is, how does she actually raise a child? What does she tell this beautiful little girl? How does she live now? Surely she doesn't pass on her expertise, does she? Because all the things she knows... Well, she wants more for her little girl, more than the dubious honor of drinking boys under the table and being the reigning blowjob queen of the bi-state area. *That* girl isn't a mom, will never *be* a mom... because, deep down, she's far too shallow, far too fake to be anything real.

"I... try to tell this chick about my old ex and his phoenix philosophies. I tell her all about it, but while you and I might be able to remake ourselves each day... we can only do that if we know who we are, who we want to be. And... this girl? She... doesn't."

Awkward silence filled the room. I could tell that Daniel didn't know what to say. From my angle, I could see the color rising in Tracy's cheeks.

I couldn't leave them hanging there, so I decided to make my entrance. I stepped out from behind the potted tree I'd been standing beside, and said, "Sorry I'm late."

Bending down, I kissed Tracy's cheek. I pulled out a chair and sat and pretended that I had no idea what was going on. I don't like to brag, but I have a very particular set of skills, skills I have acquired over a lifetime. One of those skills, perhaps my number one skill, in fact, is the ability to convincingly appear to have no idea what's going on.

Some would call me a natural.

"So... Where's Tony?" I said.

Daniel looked down at the plate of pickled seaweed salad in front of him. "...He didn't come."

"Oh," I said. "Well, that's a shame. This place makes a mean Mapo Doufu." I grinned. It was the clueless grin of a guy unaware of the big ole Jacuzzi of awkward he was currently stewing in. Tracy's hand found mine and squeezed a little, a signal designed to shut me up.

I turned toward her. "Faith's with your parents?"

She nodded. I could see the slightest trace of color in her cheeks, a remnant of the embarrassment that surged through her when I'd shown up. I was sorry for that, but not for what I'd overheard. Sometimes spying worked. Just ask the NSA.

Things never really warmed up, even with a table full of excellent, albeit thermonuclear, Sichuan food. The awkwardness remained, as if I'd walked in on the two of them having sex instead of just talking. I wasn't all that worried about it. In the last few years I've been in some seriously uncomfortable spots. Spots that made this shit look like a Disney vacation.

"How are the legs?" I asked Daniel halfway through the meal. The owner had brought over a free round of beers. While it was true that I was attempting to be better about my drinking, I happily accepted and thanked her profusely. It would've been rude to do otherwise.

He nodded, took a sip of beer, and said, "Sore, but okay."

That was good. Whatever was going on with Daniel, I didn't think it was physical, at least, not entirely. Sometimes injury changes a person. Sometimes it's the brush with mortality, but what I'd seen a lot of, as an acupuncturist – the last, desperate attempt of the person who has done everything else they could think of – was that pain, chronic pain, was a machinery, an ever-turning millstone that ground away at your reserves. It sapped whatever strength you once had until all that was left was the constant, unwanted ache, an unwelcome companion telling you that you were weak, worthless, done. If the pain was bad enough, or constant enough, you'd do just about anything to make it stop. The alternative was going crazy.

"So what's the problem, then?" I said. I dropped the phony, clueless smile.

Daniel froze, chopsticks poised over his plate. "W-What?"

"What is it that Tony's done that's got you so messed up?"

He looked to Tracy, who again gave my hand a squeeze – a warning squeeze this time.

"Look," I said, "I overheard some of what you said. I wasn't trying to, but it just happened. So why don't we just drop all the bullshit and talk? I'm here to *help* you, Daniel."

He set his chopsticks down and adjusted the napkin on the table, looking as though he wasn't sure if he wanted to tell me what was up... or throw hot soup at my face. Either would have been a reasonable response, but I was hoping for answers, mostly because I really did want to help him but also because I like my face best when it is unburned by soup.

Tracy slid in closer – always a welcome response – and said, "Randall... Tony gave Lawrence Lim a promotion."

The way she said it, I felt like that should've meant something, but I had no idea who Lawrence Lim was, what he did, or that he'd done it well enough to get promoted. That must've shown on my face, though, because she quickly added, "Um... the guy you used to call 'Oddjob.'"

I thought about it a second and the realization finally hit me. Lim had been with Daniel when we had first met. He was another one of Tony's bodyguards, and–

Shit.

I looked at Daniel and saw the pain in his eyes.

"You think he's replaced you," I said.

He looked away.

"I am," he said, carefully keeping his voice neutral, "no longer of use as the director of personal security for Mr. Lau."

I laughed. "'*Mister* Lau?'"

They stared at me with surprised, scornful faces.

"*Randall*," Tracy said, her voice very cold.

"Tony's a practical dude, Daniel. What'd you think, that he'd just keep you on the job, in the shape you're in? Of course not. He's right."

I felt Tracy's nails dig into the flesh of my arm. I put my hand on top of hers and said, "You're in no shape to protect anybody. Not while you're recovering... Nobody would be. You think he did this because he *doesn't* care about you? Daniel, he wants you back. We all do."

He looked up at me, red-rimmed eyes defiant. "I do not care that he replaced me."

"...You don't?" I said.

"I care that he still says things like, ' When you come back...' and 'Once you're on your feet again...'"

He smiled a cruel smile, grinding his teeth, the muscles rippling just beneath the skin. "I care that you – and everybody else – say that you 'want me back.' I'm *here. This is what I am now, and we can all stop pretending that I will ever be anything else. What I am, all that I am, is a fighter and I will never fight again. You know this. *He* knows this. Everything I've worked for my entire life is *gone*. Do you understand that? *Do you know what it is like to lose everything? To lose yourself?"*

The restaurant seemed unnaturally still, like time had stopped, like the world waited for an answer. I held his gaze, tinged though it was with something like triumph, something like insanity, and I finished my beer. As I set the bottle on the tablecloth, I said, "Yeah. I do. The great thing about lost stuff, though? It's still out there, somewhere... you just have to find it."

His face didn't change, but his voice did. Something there cracked just a little, and what was left was softer somehow. "H-How?" he said.

"However you can," I said. "You just... *do*. Because out of all the shitty choices you have, it's the only one that works. So you look at what you've got and maybe all you've got is the air that goes in and out of your lungs, but that's something. So you start

54

there. And from there you crawl and you drag yourself until you can stand, and once you can stand you fucking start walking. That's what you do."

I felt Tracy's hand beneath mine, the skin cool and soft, the nails long and perfectly smooth. I said, "And you have to keep your eyes open. Because while you're looking for the things you think you want, it's really easy to miss something even better. Something that's right there."

I glanced over at her, at those huge, dark eyes. When I looked back at Daniel, the softness had found its way into his muscles, easing his jaw loose, making his face look slack, lost.

"And what if it's all just gone? What about the things that are gone forever?" he said.

I saw Miranda, the way she used to duck her head into my office on her way out the door in the morning. She would hold Grace and the two of them would lean in, grinning. "Say 'bye-bye' to daddy!"

Gracie would stretch her arms out to me, one last hug before school.

"Bye-bye, Daddy! Bye-bye!"

"They're never really gone," I said, though I felt the loss so keenly in that moment that I thought it might kill me.

It didn't. It never does.

But Daniel had won. My attempts to placate him were done, all my supposed wisdom gone in a single moment.

Then silence, the stillness smothering us again as the lunch rush was over, the businessmen and families and stay-at-home moms all long gone.

Silence, except for the sound of chewing.

I looked to my left and saw Cheng, who must've appeared in the midst of our discussion and casually cracked open a Styrofoam container, oblivious to everything that had taken place. As I watched, he used his chopsticks to pass food from his container onto everyone's plates. It was the sort of thing parents did for their kids. Tracy smiled and nodded a thanks before adjusting her chopsticks, picking up a piece, and popping it into her mouth.

Almost immediately, and in a decidedly un-ladylike manner, she spat the food back onto her plate, wiped at her tongue with a napkin, and shot Cheng the most heartbreakingly hurt and betrayed look I'd ever seen.

Cheng looked offended.

"You eat," he said. "It is good for you."

After draining the rest of her drink in a (futile) effort to mask the mystery food's flavor, she growled, "No, thank you."

I looked down at my plate, took a bite, and frowned. It was a fairly traditional lamb and vegetable dish, a little salty, maybe, but it wasn't bad. In fact, there was something comforting about it, something that reminded me of home a little.

I looked at Tracy and raised an eyebrow. Cheng said, "Very American problem."

"What is?" I said.

Cheng popped a piece of vegetable into his mouth and managed to smear a bit of gravy on his lip. "In America, everything is sugar. Everything must be sweet for people to eat it. You put syrup of corn in your bread! Honey on vegetables! You wonder why so many are so fat..."

Tracy rolled her eyes. The mood had changed completely, but it was both so sudden and so subtle that I didn't quite see it at the time. We had been expertly deflected by a bit of culinary Tai Chi.

"Look, you can talk shit about Americans if you want, but I don't eat like that. And even if I did... Dude, that tastes like celery dipped in molten ear wax."

"You joke, but I am serious. This is a very serious American problem," Cheng said, blinking. "Not just food. You spread it throughout the world now, the food and the problems."

"What the hell are you talking about?" Tracy said. "And what the hell *was* that? My tongue is numb from it..."

I realized then what it was that she'd tasted. *Ku gua* – bitter melon – was a popular culinary ingredient and herbal medicine. I guess it was something of an acquired taste, but I'd grown up on the stuff.

"The way you approach food is the way you approach life. You think you have the luxury to pick and choose, but life is not this way. Eating too much sugar dulls your senses and rots your teeth." He gestured with chopsticks holding up a thick slice of bitter melon and said, "If you do not eat bitterness you can never truly know sweetness."

I looked at Cheng and I understood.

It was a term every martial artist knew by heart in China.

Chi ku. To eat bitterness.

Getting up at four a.m., showering in ice cold water because there was no heat, and practicing stance training for hours when it felt like bone and sinew could snap and, worse still, that the cracking of bone and the tearing of muscle might actually be a relief. The later assertion that pain was all that was, the natural state of things, and that complaining about it was as pointless as being annoyed at the constant sound of one's own heartbeat. The ultimate realization that the sensation, the one that repelled you at first, was only a sensation, that pain was a state which could be experienced without all the messy emotional baggage; the knowledge that pain wouldn't kill you. Whatever the discomfort, it became possible to see it, to accept it, to take it in, and to move on.

Chi ku.

We had become quite adept at eating bitterness. All of us. While Tracy fought against what she saw as an unfair stereotyping of Americans, I knew that wasn't really what Cheng was doing, not really. He knew we had suffered, and he sympathized, in his way. In his world, though, all of this was unseemly, much like Tracy's breach of etiquette after tasting the bitter melon.

When life handed you lemons, you ate them with a smile, peel and all, because the ability to suffer, to endure, and to press on was a virtue. If you trained yourself to be unshakeable in trivial times – the eating of lemons, the standing of stances – the hope was that you could count on yourself to persevere when life really decided to be a dick. When it handed you cancer, say, or when it abducted your child.

I, for one, had had enough of bitterness. It had scourged my tongue until I wasn't sure I would taste anything else, ever again.

Cheng had somehow talked Tracy into trying the dish again. This time he leaned over the table, feeding her a slice of lamb with a microscopic sliver of bitter melon. She took it, chewing warily, and made a face as she swallowed.

"See?" Cheng said.

"No," Tracy said. "It's still horrible. That taste just hangs in the back like a grody pervert and gets its funk all over everything else. Ugh. So gross."

Cheng's eyes twinkled. "How much better will ice cream taste now, eh?"

Tracy stared at him completely unimpressed. "I can't stand you. You know that, right? Are you coming to the wedding? Randall told you, right? You're coming, right? I'm going to make sure that every dish at the reception is a syrupy sweet mess, just for you."

I felt myself smile.

I looked across the table at Daniel and saw that, as he watched the two of them bicker, he smiled too.

***

"We should talk."

It was after our lunch, and Tracy had decided to ride along when I took Cheng back to the apartment. (It was now *the* apartment in my mind and no longer *my* apartment. I was a man without a country, a man without an apartment, a wandering, wave-tossed soul with nothing but a fat bank account and a penchant for dramatically talking about himself in the third person. Woe is me.)

In the grand scheme of things, there are theoretically worse things a woman can say to a man, even if I can't actually think of any at this moment, but 'we should talk' is sort of the conversational equivalent of sirens and flashing lights in your rearview mirror.

We picked neutral territory, because I didn't really want to have our Talk with either Cheng or Tracy's parents around. Hell, even Tito's judgmental glares were a bit much for me to take right then. We were still stuffed from lunch, so I drove down the street to Millar Park and followed Tracy to the playground. She sat on a swing and gestured for me to do the same. I initially protested on the grounds that I'm not five years old, but she gave me The Look.

I sat and tried not to really swing, but in the awkward silence that was tough. I fidgeted. And may have, inadvertently, swung a bit. Slowly.

Tracy turned to me and said, "Is this really what you want?"

"What?" I said, thinking for a brief moment that she meant the swings.

"Getting married. Is this for real, or was it all a scheme to nail McGarrity?"

I nearly jumped off the swing and crouched down at her feet. "Of course it's for real. Trace... Don't you remember the first time I asked you? There was no McGarrity."

"No, there was just me and a surprise pregnancy. So I'll ask you again: Is this what you want? Because whether it's all part of some revenge fantasy or an attempt to make everything cool with my super-Catholic parents I can handle the truth. I just need to know what that is."

She looked tired, and that was probably my fault.

"This whole exasperated thing you've got going on... are you sure you want to marry *me?* I mean, I'd be willing to bet you never made this face before we met and now you're, like, practically a pro."

She laughed without much humor and leaned against the swing's chain. "The truth, Randall. Please?"

"Yes."

She blinked. "Um... to which one?"

I sighed. "Of course I want to marry you. And not for your parents and not for revenge and not because of Faith. Not for society or tradition or some illusory ownership over you, either. I want to marry you because I can't handle the thought of not marrying you. I realize that it's modern times and we could just as easily live together or whatever, but the idea of it all... it still means something to me. And I'm sorry that I didn't tell you about McGarrity at first... but I didn't want you to worry."

She looked down at our hands. I wasn't sure when they'd come together, but there they were.

"Randall," she said quietly, "I don't want you to go after him. If that was the whole reason for Hong Kong, then I'd rather not go."

I kissed the tip of her nose.

"I picked Hong Kong because I wanted to symbolically shove it in his face and say that he didn't beat us. We survived it all and we're better than ever..."

It was a lie, but it was a harmless lie.

"...And because I wanted to take you to my favorite dumpling stand, and take you on the cable car ride up to Victoria peak. There's a whole side of me that you've never seen, and I thought maybe it was time you met that guy."

She squinted up at me and smiled. I stood up to block the sun that was blinding her. Still shading her eyes, she said, "I'd love to meet that guy. One thing, though, Randall... I think I have to keep my name. 'Tracy Lee' sounds like an eighties hair metal singer or something."

I didn't know what that was.

We talked more about details, and I sensed that she still wasn't completely sure how to take the whole situation. I didn't blame her. It's not like I *haven't* done incredibly stupid stuff behind her back before. There wasn't anything I could do about that now. All I could do was promise to include her in everything from here on out. Every plan, however dumb. Every scheme, however lame.

That's what marriage is all about.

Later, once Faith was in bed and Tito was perched atop the bedroom bookcase glaring down at us for allowing his food bowl to get half empty, I took Tracy in my arms and kissed her softly. For so long I hadn't been able to get this close to her, and I'd learned never to take it for granted.

It was a wonderful moment, her hands in my hair, the silk of her lips on my neck, the feel of her body against mine. The heat of her, the feel of her heart... What can I say? I had to ruin it.

"I think you'll definitely be the Cool Wife," is what I said.

"What?" she said, pulling back to look me in the eyes.

"The Cool Girlfriend can totally be the Cool Wife... *and* the Cool Mom. Because you're cool."

And I smiled.

I *smiled.*

Idiot.

Tracy took a step back, disentangling from me.

"So... you heard all that?"

I still smiled. I think it was stuck on my face.

"Hm?" I said.

"You were listening. That whole time. You were listening to what I said to Daniel."

"Well, I wasn't listening exactly, but I heard. Yes, I heard it...Yeah."

What surprised me was that she wasn't angry at me for having eavesdropped.

She was ashamed.

Before I could manage to unstick my lips, she was in tears.

"I just… I thought I could talk to Daniel because he doesn't have kids and I thought that maybe he wouldn't judge."

"…Okay," I said. I had my arm around her but she refused to be comforted.

"Randall, you know I love her, right? You *know* that, right?"

"Faith? Of course I do."

She sniffled and held her hands to her eyes and barely stifled a sob.

"Do you?" I said.

"What?"

"Do *you* know that you love her? Because it didn't sound like it from the way you were talking. I'm glad to know how you feel. I always want to know how you feel… but the things you were worried about? About how to be a mom? If you could see yourself when you're with her, you'd know. You don't have to craft some identity like a mask that you slip on and off, you don't have to try. Who you are is more than enough. You love her and you're everything to her."

She took a deep breath and tried to collect herself.

"Randall, I have a half naked woman tattooed on my thigh."

"Yes, you do. It's very nice." I caught myself. "The tattoo and the thigh."

"At various points during the time we've been together I have had fourteen different parts of my body pierced."

"That many? Wow."

"I used to have purple streaks in my hair," she said with a wistful sigh. "I *miss* having purple streaks in my hair…"

"Me too. I miss your purple streaks, I mean. I don't think I could carry that off, myself."

"You're missing the point, Randall," she said in a way that told me that this wasn't remotely the first time. "What kind of mother sports a mile of ink and purple hair?"

"Oh! Wait, I know this one…" I closed my eyes and silently mouthed out the words until I had it right. "That's called a… a 'milf,' right?"

I opened my eyes in time to see her scowl.

"I'm serious, Randall."

"So am I, Trace. Do you suppose you are the first tattooed and pierced mom in history?"

"...No, but it's more than just that... It's—"

"That you think you're not a good role model? That you think you've done unwholesome things?" I said.

"...Well, yeah..."

I just looked at her and, as she looked at me I could see it start to sink in.

"You're the one who's done all the really bad stuff, huh?" I said.

She averted her eyes and shrugged and mumbled something.

"What?" I said.

She slid her bare feet along the carpet. "...I said, 'Shut up' and then I called you a 'poopypants.'"

I put my arm around her again, but this time she leaned in and rested her head on my shoulder.

"You know that thing you mentioned, the thing your ex used to say?" I said.

She was still for a minute but then she nodded. She was probably wondering if I was going to go full jackass and get all jealous and stupid as I am wont to do.

I said, "I don't think he was quite right."

She looked up at me, eyes and nose all puffy and red from crying and still the most beautiful girl in the whole world.

"We don't have to create ourselves each night, or each day, or every third Sunday. We create ourselves every moment. Everything else is just bullshit we tell ourselves about who we are. The Tracy Sandoval I met in my shop a few years ago and the Tracy Sandoval that rocked our daughter to sleep an hour ago is the same person. It's all you, facets of the same jewel, and I wouldn't have it any other way. Faith is lucky to have you for a mom."

"But what about when she's a teenager? What kind of a role model am I going to be?"

"Why, because you'll have taught her how to express herself? Or that a woman can be whatever the hell she wants to be? Or that it's possible to be smart *and* sexy *and* kind? I'm not really seeing the downside here, Trace..."

She sniffled and regarded me seriously. "How is it that you can be so dense sometimes and then turn around and say the exact right thing at the exact right time?"

I grinned and said, "Ancient Chinese secret?"

Which, it turned out, was not the exact right thing to say.

But I still went to bed that night with the girl of my dreams, so it's not all bad.

***

The next morning, after breakfast, Tracy and Faith came with me to the shop. We went early so that I could process my latest herb shipment, which involved weighing and portioning out various herbs, and so that I would have enough time to warm up before Daniel showed up.

If he showed up. That part was still up in the air.

While I stretched, Tracy fed Faith. After, Tracy carefully lay her down in her pumpkin seat, all milk drunk and dozing, and came over to join me.

"Do you still practice the form?" I asked.

"Here and there. Not like I should," she said.

"Show me," I said. I stood back and watched while she moved slowly through the first section of the Tai Chi form, hesitating when she would forget where to go next.

"Step forward with your right foot," I said, when she got stuck on a particular posture.

"No, your other right foot," I said a moment later.

She growled at me and then complied. "What do I do with my hands?"

I moved in close behind her, put my hands over hers, and guided her through the movement. "See? It's a deflection and then a counter-attack."

"Hm," she said.

I felt her back arch and she pressed her body against me in a way that was not in accordance with the ten essential principals of Tai Chi. I cleared my throat and backed away to watch her complete her form. She cast a devilish grin in my direction before pivoting into the next posture.

"Can I ask you something, Randall?" she said.

"Of course."

"If Dim Mak is a thing, how is it that people don't accidentally 'death touch' each other all the time? Like, your bus hits a bump and you get jostled into somebody and you accidentally make their liver implode or something?"

I grinned, stepped in and corrected the position of her palm and, as she continued, said, "It's not that easy. Most strikes are combinations of points and it's not just that... Certain points have to be hit at a particular depth or a certain angle... or triggered in sequence with very particular timing... It's kind of complicated."

She said, "Oh," but with disappointment.

"Why?" I said.

She shrugged and I put my hands on her shoulders to help get her back into the proper posture. "I dunno. Just wondering, I guess. That, and I wouldn't want to hurt anybody on accident."

I walked around in front of her, close, and mirrored her stance.

"Do you remember Pushing Hands?" I said.

She winced and said, "...Sorta?"

I walked her through the basic exercise until we were comfortably moving, slowly, rhythmically. When she knew the movements fairly well, I started to show her some applications. She needed to know that there was more, so much more, to the art than what I had shown her. She needed to see that it wasn't about hurting people.

The doorbell jingled just as she put me into an immobilizing elbow lock. I had to crane my neck to see that it was Daniel. He nodded a greeting my way and, to Tracy, said, "Torque that joint good. He deserves it."

***

I don't know what changed. I don't know if Daniel even knows what changed. I'd like to think that it was something I said, or that the practice and treatments started helping enough with his pain, or even that he and Tony worked things out, but something had brought back the fight in him. And while he was more than willing to give me as much shit as humanly possible every step of the way, he stopped fighting my instruction.

He stopped using his cane, even though I advised him to use it a little bit longer. I don't want to give the impression that there was some miraculous recovery here. There wasn't. There was no magic; Daniel fought and clawed for every achievement, however small. Sometimes he pushed himself too far.

Our trip was a few months away. There was still so much left to do. Once my clientele (the ones who hadn't given up on me already for being the most unreliable acupuncturist in the St. Louis area) got wind that I was going out of town – again – my schedule filled up unexpectedly. Practice time with Daniel got pushed back first to late afternoon, then to evening.

Cheng started helping out with patients, which was weird in itself, but the fact that he did it without being asked was unprecedented. Then he started hanging out during Daniel's practice times, occasionally jumping in to correct Daniel (or me), but often just sitting and watching. Sometimes he brought snacks.

We started practicing in the park again. Once the shop was closed for the evening there were still a few hours of daylight and, usually, the day's temperature would have cooled to something resembling comfortable. More and more often, Tracy would come, too, and I always had to wonder if the small crowd of spectators who gathered was there to see the beauty and grace of Tai Chi or to ogle my fiancé's ass.

Daniel pestered Tony into joining. Then we talked Knox into coming out. Sometimes Marta would join us, and she and Tracy would chat beneath the trees and play with Faith while the rest of us enjoyed the manly art of moving really slow for fun and profit.

Things were feeling good again. It was starting to be less like the broken veterans of unpopular wars being rehabilitated and more like old friends getting together to enjoy each other's company.

I found that I no longer had time anymore to focus on my countless past failings. There was already too much pain in the world to keep holding so tightly to old hurts. Not that they just disappeared. I still had the nightmares sometimes, but most of the time I was just too damned tired to dream.

The sun was low in the sky and the fireflies had begun to dance their constellations along the horizon. It was getting too dark to practice, and Knox had already suggested dinner, when one of the spectators – we typically had a small, revolving, but pretty consistent crowd now whenever we practiced – approached slowly.

"Dr. Lee?" he said. I didn't immediately recognize the young African-American man who stood before me. He was taller by at least a few inches, and he'd packed a lot of muscle onto what was once a very lean frame. He'd grown up a lot since I'd seen him last.

"David?" I said at last. He smiled. I wasn't sure I'd ever seen the kid smile before. Of course, when I'd last seen him, he hadn't had much to smile about. David's best friend was one of the first victims of McGarrity's jade… Darnell Stevens, the kid who had nearly killed Knox.

We shook hands. I invited him to dinner. He declined, but asked if he could talk to me privately. I walked him away from the rest of the group, near the oak where Tracy and Marta sometimes sat. He stared down at the ground uncomfortably. I was about to press him when he pulled a piece of paper out of his pocket and handed it to me.

"I…uh… wanted to let you know that I graduated in the spring. And… that… I just found out that I got accepted to the police academy," he said.

I looked up at him. "…Wow. That's great, David."

Since I'd had to strip a pistol from his hand when we first met, I was more than a little surprised, but it was a pleasant surprise. He clearly knew what I was thinking because he said, "It's weird, right? Who would've thought I'd end up being a cop, right?"

I smiled and folded his acceptance letter to hand to him. "I think it's pretty awesome."

He got uncomfortable again, and I didn't understand why. He stuffed the letter back in his jeans pocket and shrugged.

"Thing is, Dr. Lee… You gave me the idea."

I stared at him. "What?"

"Well, maybe not directly. I don't mean like that. It was more of the way that you just… gave a fuck."

I kept on staring. "…Okay," I said.

David Morris took a breath and said, "Look, I never knew what I was going to do. I almost didn't care as long as I got the hell away from here, y'know?"

I nodded.

"Man, all that stuff with Darnell... I just couldn't handle it. Didn't want to. And when you came around, I figured you were just another asshole, y'know."

I did. I was.

"The difference between them and you, though, is that you actually gave a fuck. About Darnell, about me, about *people.* And you didn't have to. I never really got to say thanks or anything, but when I thought about it I started thinking that there's some shit that a thanks doesn't cover..."

"Hey, David–" I started, but he interrupted me.

"No. *This* is my thanks to you, man. I can't pay you back... there's no way to. But I can pay it forward, y'know?"

I nodded.

There's a line in the Tao Te Ching that came to mind. Like most of the other lines, it was tough to translate, but the essence (or, at least, how I understand it) is something like, "Just do your work and let it go." I realized a long time ago the wisdom in that simple line because, in life, you can never really know the mark you make on the world. Each word, each act, even just being there... Sometimes – hell, most of the time – we'll never know just how important those moments are to someone else. And David was right. Something like that, the seemingly minute but ineffable kindness may only be a drop in the bucket, but that drop produces ripples that spread outward in unpredictable ways.

There's a picture I keep up on my wall. It's a crayon drawing by a little girl who saw me as a superhero.

I do not feel like a superhero. Most of the time I feel like a sad excuse for an asshole.

Whether I see myself as a good man or a bad man doesn't really matter. At the end of the day, I am just a man. How I feel about it doesn't matter.

What I *do* matters.

And I've found that what I do is endure. I try my best to keep going, to do my work and let it go. Sometimes, like today, I get to see the fruits of my labors, and it surprises me when I realize that they are never bitter.

There would always be mysteries, countless things in life that I did not or could not know, but of one thing I was absolutely certain: Whatever David's bullshit reasons were for trying to duck out of dinner with the rest of us, they were sure to be weak and easily deflectable.

The group of us – all of us – went to Joy Luck and ordered hotpot. This time there were no goofy shows of machismo, just excellent food and excellent drink and beyond excellent company.

I saw Knox with his arm around David, telling him stories about his time in the academy. Cheng cradled Faith in the crook of one arm while goading Marta Knox to eat more, "For baby! For baby!" Daniel and Tony sat very near each other and, although Daniel wore the same steely mask I'd seen when we first met, I couldn't help but notice that the two of them were openly holding hands. That, as far as I knew, was new.

I reached out for Tracy's hand and she turned.

"Okay?" she said.

I nodded. "I just wanted to hold your hand."

She flashed her radiant smile, kissed me, and turned back to her conversation with Tony. As she did so, she tucked a strand of newly dyed, vibrant purple hair behind her ear.

I resisted the urge to nip at her exposed neck because, apparently, I am a Zen master.

Sitting back and nursing a glass of iced tea, I watched our loud, chaotic gathering. More than friends, we were a family forged out of tragedy and horror and desperation. We had fought against each other, for each other, and detained each other (legally and otherwise). We'd broken each other and we'd built each other back up. In a few instances we'd tried to kill each other and, thankfully, found that, so far at least, we pretty much sucked at that. We had seen the worst of what there was to see, and we had come through it all, more or less.

Sharing a simple meal with what I truly regarded as my family, I felt a tremendous sense of gratitude for all that we had been through, and endured, together. We had eaten bitterness, only to find that it tasted sweet.

Epilogue

The man in black arrived unnoticed. There was no particular skill to it, no stealth, only a simplicity to his features, something utterly common in his bearing, that told everyone he met that there was no point in paying any attention to him. He moved through the hospital's halls swiftly, decisive movement masking the need to quickly scan the signs on the walls.

The morgue was easy enough to find.

He slipped inside. If this had been a normal case, the man in black would have been forced to hack into the hospital computers and skim through dozens of files to find the particular corpse he was looking for.

This was no normal case.

The man in black began checking the cold chambers. The first few he checked were unusable, bodies mangled in an automobile collision at the site of the most recent incident. The third refrigerator drawer he opened yielded results, however.

The man in black pried open the corpse's eyelids, exposing rust-colored sclerae and yellowed irises. He took a smartphone from his pocket, opened the camera app, and took several photos before sliding the drawer back and closing the thick metal door.

He checked the occupants of several other drawers only to find similar – or worse – damage. He photographed them all and forwarded the photos back to his home in a text message.

A response came in moments. The text, written in traditional *hanzi*, read "You are certain?"

The man in black wrote that it was indisputable.

Indisputable and inexcusable.

While the others bickered among themselves, the man in black *knew*. The trail, once seen, was simple to follow. And while the others chose to believe that this aberration was a recent phenomenon, the man in black had followed the trail back and back, tracing the transgressions as they spread from place to place, from year to year.

The Art was here, in America.

And it was being perverted.

He opened one final drawer and felt his professional detachment quaver. This corpse was worse than any of the others, worse than anything he had ever seen. Much of the man's skull appeared fleshless, his eyes ragged and lidless. The man in black had no answer for what had happened to the man's face, but one look at the corpse's ruptured abdomen told him that this poor soul was yet another victim.

He took photos of the wound and sent them along with the message, "It is time to act."

As the youngest member of the Order, it was perhaps unwise to risk impertinence, but enough was enough.

The drawer was closed, its horrors once again hidden, and the morgue vacated before their reply came. The man in black could just picture the old fools nattering back and forth, unable even now to make a decision.

He was halfway to his car when he felt the phone vibrate silently in his pocket.

"Agreed." The message read. "Find him."

The man in black smiled.

Because while the Order bickered among themselves over what was considered proof, over what was considered a transgression, over whether or not there could be more than one transgressor (an idiotic thought if ever he'd heard one), and over countless other moronic trivialities, the man in black already *had* found him.

Once inside his nondescript sedan, the man in black programmed his GPS for the city of Saint Louis and started the engine.

So, What's Next for Randall and Tracy?

The Art of War (Coming Soon)

Stay up to date with Randall Lee's adventures, and my other projects, by signing up to my newsletter! It's fast, it's free, and I promise not to bomb your inbox with lots of junk. Send an email to charlescolyott@gmail.com. Be sure to write "Newsletter" in the subject line. Members will receive exclusive news, previews of new books, and, quite possibly, some free stuff!

Support Indie Writers!

If you enjoyed this book, please tell your friends! Word of mouth and good reviews are crucial for new and indie writers. A quick review on Amazon, a mention on Goodreads or even a shared link on Facebook can mean a lot to get the word out about the books you love!

About the Author

Charles Colyott lives on a farm in the middle of nowhere (Illinois) with his wife, 2 daughters, cats, and a herd of llamas and alpacas. He is surrounded by so much cuteness it's very difficult for him to develop any street cred as a dark and gritty writer. Nevertheless, he has appeared in *Read by Dawn II*, Dark Recesses Press, *Withersin* magazine, *Horror Library* Volumes III & IV, *Terrible Beauty*, *Fearful Symmetry*, and *Zippered Flesh*, among other places. He also teaches a beginner level Tai Chi Ch'uan class in which no one has died (yet) of the death touch.

You can get in touch with him on Facebook, or email him at charlescolyott@gmail.com.

Unlike his llamas, he does not spit.

Made in the USA
Middletown, DE
25 March 2022